Money Train

Danny Spence plans to stay in Gila Creek for only one night, but then he gets mistaken for a snake named Zeke Tolan, and from then on it is just one damn thing after another.

He falls foul of the evil Ma Cole, gets himself on the wrong side of the vicious Hernando Ortiz and his sadistic bodyguard Bracho – and somehow this is all wrapped up with a train full of money that's rolling south of the border, right into the middle of the Mexican revolution.

By the same author

South to Sonora
Tanner's Revenge

Money Train

Michael Stewart

A Black Horse Western

ROBERT HALE

© Michael Stewart 2019
First published in Great Britain 2019

ISBN 978-0-7198-2897-3

The Crowood Press
The Stable Block
Crowood Lane
Ramsbury
Marlborough
Wiltshire SN8 2HR

www.bhwesterns.com

Robert Hale is an imprint
of The Crowood Press

Typeset by
Derek Doyle & Associates, Shaw Heath
Printed and bound in Great Britain by
4Bind Ltd, Stevenage, SG1 2XT

For Sarah

CHAPTER ONE

When Danny Spence rode into town that hot Arizona afternoon, he didn't expect to stay long. He was just passing through on the way to the ocean.

He'd spent almost his whole life in Texas, but he'd read about the ocean since he was a kid, and had a hankering to see it. So now, with a few dollars in his pocket after his last cattle drive, he was heading west to California.

Spence's plan was, he'd spend a night or two here in Gila Creek, rest his horse, rest his bones, maybe even get himself a bath, then move on.

He didn't notice the man outside the Pot O'Gold saloon looking at him funny.

Nor did he notice the two women outside the general store looking at him funny.

Nor did he notice the kid outside the rooming house looking at him funny, then run and fetch the sheriff.

Spence found the livery stable and said to the old

7

man who ran the place, 'I'm planning to stay in town a day or two. You got room for my horse?'

The man was way past sixty, thin as a rail and with a bushy grey beard. He stared at Spence, his mouth hanging open.

Spence reckoned the man might be a little deaf, so he said it again.

The man swallowed a couple of times, his eyes wide, and said, 'Sure. Sure we have. I – I got room.'

Spence had met fellows before who stammered, and he'd met men who went through life so scared they were frightened of their own shadows, so he didn't think anything of it, he just handed the man the reins of his horse and said, 'How much?'

The man stammered some more and told him how much it would be, so Spence got the roll of money from his pocket and paid the man in advance.

The man stared at the roll of money. Then he stared at the banknote Spence was holding out to him, like he was scared to take it. A dribble of sweat trickled down his forehead, past his eye, and disappeared into his beard.

Mighty peculiar, thought Spence. He'd never seen anybody so reluctant to take money.

'Are you all right?' asked Spence.

The man swallowed again, then his hand darted out like a rattlesnake and grabbed the banknote.

Spence nodded, said, 'Nice doing business with you,' took his saddle-bags and strolled over to the rooming house.

There was a group of people gathered outside the general store. The two women who'd been looking at him funny as he'd rode by had been joined by two other women, and a man who'd been buying supplies in there, and by the owner of the store. All six of them saw Spence as he emerged from the livery stable, and quickly looked away. As he walked past he saw one of the woman sneak a peek at him, so he tipped his hat and said, 'Good day, Ma'am,' and she looked away again, like he'd said something dirty. The rest of the group were either staring at their feet, or had found something interesting to look at in the distance, and all of their mouths were set in grim little lines.

Spence shrugged and carried on to the rooming house.

The woman behind the desk was a little over twenty, Spence guessed, in a cotton print dress and with her blonde hair piled up on top of her head.

'I'd like a room,' he told her, taking off his hat.

She didn't stare at him or stammer or anything, just smiled and said, 'Sure,' and plucked a key off the row of hooks behind her.

After he'd handed over another of one of his hard-earned banknotes he said, 'You get many strangers here in Gila Creek?'

'All the time,' she said. 'Why? You looking for some-body?'

'It ain't that,' Spence said. 'It's just that when I was in the livery stable just now, the old fellow in there acted like he was plumb scared of me. Didn't even

9

want to take my money.'

She laughed. 'That's just old Pete. I shouldn't pay any mind to him. He's good with horses, but around people he's just about the jumpiest critter this side of El Paso.'

'That ain't all, though. A bunch of folks outside the general store were watching me as I left the livery stable. They pretended they weren't, but they were, and when I said good day to one of 'em, she looked like I'd cussed at her. It all seems mighty strange.'

She laughed again. But then she looked past him, out of the window, and she stopped laughing.

'What is it?' Spence asked. But she didn't reply, she just carried on looking out of the window, a frown creasing her forehead.

Spence turned his head to see what she was looking at. There was a crowd of people on the opposite side of the street, all looking over at the rooming house.

The woman tore her eyes away from the window and looked at Spence again. Only now, instead of looking at him like he was a regular human being like she'd done before, she was looking at him like he was one part coyote, three parts rattlesnake.

Another thought occurred to him. 'This one of those towns where you're supposed to hand your gun over to the sheriff the moment you set foot in town? I looked for a sign, but I didn't see one.'

She shook her head. She said, 'No, it ain't one of those towns.'

'Then what. . . ?'

The door burst open and a large man with a tin badge pinned to his chest filled the doorway. He had a jaw like a locomotive's cow catcher, and a nose that had spent its whole life getting pummelled. He also had a rifle in his hands, and he was pointing it at Spence.

'You got a nerve, I'll give you that,' said the sheriff.

Spence said, 'Now Sheriff, I don't rightly know what's going on here, or if I've broken some law I didn't know about, but all I want is to. . . .'

He didn't get to finish what he was going to say because the sheriff chose that moment to swipe him across the head with the butt of his rifle, and everything went black awhile.

Spence woke up with a pain across one side of his face like he'd been branded with a hot iron. He was lying on a wooden bench inside a cell. He hauled himself off the bench and tried to stand, but the ground shifted beneath his feet and he felt sick, so he sat down on the edge of the bench and stared at the floor till his stomach settled.

A door opened and the sheriff appeared on the other side of the bars.

'So you've woken up, you sonofabitch,' said the lawman. 'That's good. I wanted to let you know, you've got one more week left to live. Judge Cruickshank will arrive in town, and he wants to see you hang as much as everybody else does. One of the folk you killed was his cousin's girl, Martha. Sixteen years old, prettiest thing I ever saw. We'll give you a fair trial, then we'll hang you real slow.'

Spence looked at the sheriff. 'I didn't kill anybody,' he said. 'You got the wrong man.'

'I got the right man, all right. I saw you myself, when your bandanna fell away from your face. Remember that? Half the town saw you. You got some nerve, coming back here. A haircut and a change of clothes don't make a damn difference. Why'd you come here? To laugh at us? It's only been three months. You think we're all so dumb we wouldn't know it was you?'

Spence said, 'My name's Daniel Spence. Three months ago I was herding cattle in Texas for a man named Buchanan. He owns the Lazy Q, outside of Amarillo. Get word to him, he'll . . .'

The sheriff was holding a bunch of keys on an iron ring. He unlocked the cell door, swung it open and stepped inside.

Spence was in no condition to defend himself. The sheriff hit him with a punch so hard it lifted him clear off the bench.

Spence crashed against the wall and sank to the floor.

'Don't rile me, boy,' said the sheriff. 'Or you'll spend your last week on Earth with a broken jaw. You're Zeke Tolan. You're a murderer and a horse thief, and I'm gonna put the noose around your neck myself.'

CHAPTER TWO

They fed him, but the food was thin soup and stale bread, and they gave him water to drink. And every day the sheriff, whose name was Pooley, told Spence how much he was going to enjoy watching him hang.

Between times, when he wasn't eating or getting jeered at by Pooley, Spence lay on the hard wooden bunk and tried to figure if there was some way he could escape.

Spence's cell was part of a larger room: stone floor and walls, and a solid ceiling. Just the one thick wooden door, a bolt on the other side, no hinges visible.

A row of floor-to-ceiling iron bars ran across the room, and another row of bars divided the cell half of the room into two.

There was a window, about a foot square, high in the outer wall, with iron bars across that too. Spence could barely reach it.

The wooden bench was securely bolted to the wall

and the floor, and the only other item in the cell was a tin chamber pot.

Spence was damned if he could see a way of getting out of there. He'd tested the bars, but they were cemented firmly in place. He'd been given a spoon to eat his soup with, but that was tin, as was the bowl, and when he tried to dig at the floor, or the wall, the spoon just bent. So that was that.

Four days after Spence had got thrown in jail, he got some company.

It was the early hours of Sunday morning. Spence had heard gunshots a little way down the street, the saloon he guessed. Gila Creek was a small town. It only had the one saloon. And a few minutes after the gunshots, the thick wooden door opened and Sheriff Pooley threw a man inside.

The man crashed into the bars of Spence's cell. Light from an oil lamp seeped into the room from beyond the door, and Spence could see that the man's forehead was bleeding. Other than that, the man was tall and wiry, with a thin face and a hook of a nose.

Sheriff Pooley opened the door of the other cell, picked the man up and threw him onto it.

The man crumpled to the floor and lay still.

'Got company for you,' said Pooley, slamming the cell door. 'Sonofabitch shot three men in the saloon. Killed two of 'em, and the other one's bleeding out. He'll be dead soon, too. Looks like we're going to have ourselves a real hanging party once Judge Cruickshank gets here. You two can hang side by side.

14

Maybe we'll hang you face to face, so you can watch each other squirm. Would you like that, Tolan?'

'I keep telling you,' said Spence, 'my name ain't Tolan. You got the wrong man.'

'Says you. Tell that to Judge Cruickshank.'

The sheriff left them alone and shut the thick wooden door. Spence heard the iron bolt slam into place.

A moment later the man in the other cell stirred. 'He gone?'

'Yeah,' said Spence.

The man got to his feet. Just enough moonlight oozed in through the high window for Spence to make him out.

The man grinned. 'My, that sheriff is a mean one. Hit me across the head with his rifle butt. That just ain't playing fair.'

'Did the same to me,' said Spence, thinking that the man didn't look as beat as he had done a moment ago. He must have been play-acting.

'I'm Abel Cole,' said the man. 'You heard of me?'

'Afraid not,' said Spence. 'Should I have?'

'Why, I'm famous,' said Cole. 'Me and my clan are the scourge of Arizona. When they hear the name Cole, grown men tremble.'

Spence wasn't sure what a 'scourge' was, but it didn't sound good.

'I ain't from round here,' said Spence. 'I'm from Texas.'

'They ain't heard of the Cole clan in Texas?' He

15

sounded disappointed.

'Maybe some folk have,' said Spence. 'But I ain't. But I've spent most of my time on cattle drives.'

'That explains it,' said Cole, sticking his hand through the bars that divided the two cells. 'Pleasure to make your acquaintance, I'm sure.'

Spence had been taught by his long-dead ma that it was only polite to shake a man's hand when he offered it to you, so he got up and shook the hand. 'I'm Daniel Spence,' he said. 'Friends call me Danny. But the sheriff seems to think I'm somebody called Zeke Tolan, and nothing I can say will persuade him otherwise.'

'Zeke Tolan?' said Cole. 'I'm guessing you ain't heard of him either?'

'I have not. Met a Zeke once, but he wasn't a Tolan.'

Cole gave a low whistle. 'If the good people of Gila Creek think you're Zeke Tolan, they're gonna hang you for sure. Then they're liable to cut you into pieces and feed you to the coyotes. Zeke Tolan's almost as big a scourge as the Coles. I heard he killed five men before he was old enough to vote. But people are prone to exaggeration. It was probably only three.'

He lay on his bench.

'You don't seem a whole lot worried about getting hanged,' said Spence.

'I ain't,' said Cole.

'How come?'

'You'll find out.'

Spence didn't know what that was supposed to

mean, and before he could ask, Cole said, 'You ever been down Mexico way?'

'No.'

'They got a revolution warming up down there. A man could get himself lost down there real easy, what with all that fighting. And the *señoritas* are the prettiest in the world. You never been kissed till you been kissed by one of them Mexican *señoritas* . . .'

And then Spence heard snoring. He peered through the bars between the two cells, through the faintly moonlit gloom, and saw that Cole was sleeping like he didn't have a care in the world.

I'll be damned, thought Spence.

He lay on the hard wooden bench and tried to get to sleep himself, but it didn't happen. Somehow the thought of getting hung in a few days' time made him kind of agitated, and he was still awake when the sky turned blue outside the high window.

The day of Judge Cruickshank's arrival came quick enough, and it wasn't quite noon before Sheriff Pooley and a couple of his deputies dragged Spence and Cole out of their cells, pinned their arms behind their backs with steel handcuffs, and hauled them down to the saloon.

In the street, immediately outside the doors of the saloon, the townsfolk had erected a gallows, with two nooses strung over the crossbar.

Inside, they'd pushed most of the tables over to the side of the room and arranged the chairs into rows.

17

The judge sat behind a table at the end of the saloon furthest the door, his back to the wall. He was a bald, burly fellow in his sixties with thick grey eyebrows stuck onto a face that was a mass of burst blood vessels, red as a beet.

Spence had only ever once met a man with a face that colour. That man had spent all of his waking hours working himself up into a rage about one thing or another, so Spence had reckoned it was the anger that was the cause. Judge Cruickshank looked like he had much the same temperament.

When the two of them got pushed through the swinging doors, the judge pointed at them and yelled, 'Here they are! Look at them – the scum of the Earth! Now pipe down all of you, this court is in session! Who's defending them?'

Nobody wanted to defend them, so the judge told a drunk named Walt Hardy to defend them. Hardy didn't seem to mind too much, but then he barely knew what was happening anyway. All he cared about was the jug of whiskey he was cradling in his arms.

'Which of them is Tolan?' asked Cruickshank.

'This one,' said the sheriff, pushing Spence forward into the clear space in the middle of the room.

'I ain't Tolan,' said Spence. 'My name's Daniel . . .'

The sheriff swiped him across the back of his head so hard with the flat of his hand that Spence crashed to the floor.

'What did he say?' asked the judge.

'Keeps saying he ain't Tolan,' said Sheriff Pooley.

'But it's a lie. Half the town can swear to it.'

'That so?' Cruickshank asked the crowd.

All at once just about everybody started shouting that Spence had been the man who'd led the gang that had robbed the bank three months earlier.

Spence got himself up onto his feet and said, 'It's a lie! I told this fool of a sheriff, three months ago I was herding cattle in Texas for a man named Buchanan.'

The judge's face went a deeper shade of crimson and said, 'You think we're so dumb we'll believe that? We got thirty people here who've testified they saw you rob that bank! Where's my cousin Mary Lou?'

A tall, thin woman dressed all in black with a black bonnet and veil stepped forward. 'I'm here, cousin Jake.'

The judge looked at her from underneath the unruly grey eyebrows. 'Cousin Mary Lou, you know that while this court is in session, you have to call me Your Honour.'

'I'm sorry, Your Honour.'

'That's all right, I know how deeply distressed you are, and your forgetfulness is understandable under the circumstances. Now, Mary Lou, do you see in this court the crawling snake that shot and killed your precious Martha?'

The woman pointed a bony finger at Spence. 'That's him! I was only six feet away from him, no further away than I am now! There ain't no mistake!'

The crowd started roaring. Somebody shouted, 'String him up!' Somebody else yelled, 'Stretch his neck, the sonofabitch!'

Cruickshank had a bottle of good whiskey on the table in front of him. He used it as a gavel, slamming it down on the tabletop. 'Order in court!'

The saloon quietened down. Cruickshank turned to the drunk who'd been given the job of defending Spence. 'What do you have to say, Walt?'

The man shrugged and said, 'The defence rests. I figure he should plead guilty and throw himself on the mercy of the court.'

'The hell I will!' yelled Spence. Sheriff Pooley swiped him across the back of his head again, but this time with the butt of his rifle, and once more Spence found himself lying face down in the sawdust.

The judge turned his attention to Abel Cole. His trial took even less time that Spence's, and soon the judge was yelling, 'I sentence both of these miserable varmints to hang by the neck till they're good and dead. Sentence to be carried out immediately!' The crowd erupted with whoops and cheers. Cruickshank hammered on the table again with the bottle. 'Sheriff, you got the gallows all ready?'

'Sure have, Your Honour.'

'Then get it done.'

CHAPTER THREE

A couple of the sheriff's deputies grabbed Spence's arms and hauled him out into the harsh Arizona sunlight.

The gallows, with its two nooses hanging from the crossbar, looked like some evil malformed tree, silhouetted there against the bright blue sky.

They dragged and prodded Spence up the steps to the platform and slipped a noose around his neck.

Next to him, Cole was getting the same treatment. And he didn't look so goddamn cheerful any more. Spence had seen the panic in his eyes.

Sheriff Pooley whispered in Spence's ear, 'You like our gallows, boy? We made it so we could hang up to six men at once from it. When we're not using it we keep it in a shed back of the saloon, snug and safe, and all the timbers wrapped in burlap. It's got trapdoors and everything. See, in this town, we don't just hang people from a tree. We hang 'em properly. We even got Reverend Scroggins to chant some words. Here he comes now. . . .'

A pot-bellied, rosy-cheeked, pompous-looking man was striding towards the gallows in his Sunday best, carrying a big Bible.

Reverend Scroggins climbed the steps and stood to one side of Spence and Cole.

The townspeople had worked themselves up into a frenzy. They'd poured out of the saloon and were now stood around the gallows, drinking from bottles of beer and whiskey, and competing with each other as to who could shout the foulest insults.

Judge Cruickshank had mounted the gallows. He raised his arms and yelled, 'Shut the hell up, all of you. I can scarce hear myself think! Now, before we hang these sons of bitches, Reverend Scroggins is going to speak some words from the holy book, so keep things nice and civilised. So bow your heads and pray, you bastards!'

A collective groan rose up from the crowd, but nobody dared argue, so they all bowed their heads.

The preacher started reading from the book, and Spence thought how the man sure liked the sound of his own voice. Each word boomed from his mouth clear and loud and fully formed, and rolled across the heads of the assembled townsfolk.

Spence looked around and saw the sheriff standing at the edge of the platform, his head bowed, his Stetson in his hand. His other hand rested on the lever that would release the long, narrow trapdoor that Spence and Cole were standing on.

Reverend Scroggins was getting into his stride,

reading out something about the path of righteous-ness, when the sheriff sagged, and thudded onto the scaffold's platform, and lay still. Then Spence heard the crack of a distant gunshot.

Spence saw there was a hole in the sheriff's back.

Sheriff Pooley had been shot through the heart. The bullet had entered his chest, just below the tin star, passed right through him, and burst out the other side.

Then came the first explosion.

It tore the general store apart, sending fragments of roof tile high up into the blue Arizona sky. And then as the crowd were turning to see what had happened, the sheriff's office erupted too.

Judge Cruickshank stood on the gallows and stared with his mouth open at the plume of black cloud rising up from the sheriff's ruined office. He started to say something, but whatever it was got lost, because a hole appeared in the middle of his forehead and the back of his head flew away.

By now Reverend Scroggins had realized that the gallows wasn't a safe place to be. He dropped his book and made to run for the steps, but then he got a bullet in the shoulder. He crashed through the rail, and fell awkwardly onto the ground, a jumble of arms and legs squirming in the dirt.

Then came the *rat-tat-tat* sound. Spence had never heard anything like it before. It wasn't till much later that Cole told him it was the sound of a Gatling gun, and that it was capable of firing four hundred or more rounds in a single second.

All Spence knew at the time was, the townsfolk were getting torn apart by bullets. He'd seen men get shot before, but this was different. This was a massacre. Some folk tried to make a run for it, but they didn't get far, and within seconds there was hardly a person left alive in that street, other than Danny Spence and Abel Cole up on the gallows.

The machine gun stopped its chattering, and the only sound was the whinnying of the horses in the livery stable a hundred or so yards down the street.

Spence felt sick. Next to him, Cole laughed. 'Look at 'em! The fine people of Gila Creek! Not so goddamn holier-than-thou now, are they? Almost a shame, all these pious Christian folk, dead in the street and nobody left to bury 'em. Well, let 'em rot. Let the coyotes and the vultures pick at 'em!'

Spence heard running horses. Five riders appeared from around the side of the rooming house and headed their way. When the riders got to the gallows, one of them dismounted and ran up the steps to the platform and lifted the noose away from Abel Cole's neck.

'Hey, Abel,' said the man. 'Can't you go into a town just once without shooting up the place?' The man drew out a knife and cut the rope binding Abel's wrists.

'Good to see you too, Virgil,' said Abel Cole. He turned to Spence. 'This is my brother Virgil,' he said.

'Pleased to make your acquaintance,' said Virgil.

'Likewise,' said Spence.

'Quit your jawin' and let's get out of here,' yelled another of the riders. 'Stagecoach from Tucson is due in soon.'

Spence was surprised to see that the rider who'd just yelled out was a woman, though she was dressed as a man. About fifty years old maybe, and solidly built, with the meanest eyes Spence had ever seen.

'Hey Ma,' shouted Abel. 'I've missed you!'

'I've missed you too, boy,' she replied, her thin-lipped mouth twisting into a grin. Half her teeth were missing, and the ones that were left were yellow.

Beneath her, one of the townsfolk stirred. Spence recognized the drunk, Walt Hardy, the man who'd been told to defend Spence and Cole in the saloon, though he hadn't done a damn thing. He lay in the dirt with blood oozing out of three big holes in his belly. 'Help me,' he said. 'I need a doctor . . .'

Cole's ma drew her Colt .45 and shot him in the head.

CHAPTER FOUR

Abel and Virgil were busy grinning at each other, and their ma was looking around her for more people to kill, and the other horsemen looked like they were itching to get away. Nobody was paying any mind to him at all.

'Hey,' said Spence, 'what about me?'

Ma Cole looked at him and said, 'What about you? You ain't nothing to me.'

Spence said, 'You ain't going to leave me standing here with a rope around my neck?'

One of the horsemen, thin and wiry like Abel and with the same hooked nose, grinned and said, 'You won't have to wait long for the stagecoach to get here. It's due sometime today. Of course, every now and again it gets delayed and it's a day late. You'll just have to mind you don't fall asleep.' He laughed.

Ma Cole aimed her gun at Spence's head. 'Maybe I should shoot you now. I reckon it ain't never a good thing to leave witnesses. Not if I can help it.'

Abel said, 'Aw, come on, Ma! This fellow here kept me company these last few days. We're old friends.'

'So?' asked Ma. Her gun hadn't wavered. It was still pointed at Spence's head. 'I ain't carrying any dead weight.'

Then another of the horsemen, not the one who'd spoken up before – this one was a little bulkier, but had the same hooked nose – said, 'What they want to hang you for, anyway?'

Before Spence could reply, Abel said, 'They reckoned he was Zeke Tolan, though he told 'em he wasn't.'

Ma's forehead creased up as she studied him. 'That right? You Zeke Tolan?'

Spence thought about what she'd said about not carrying dead weight, and reckoned she might not shoot him if she thought he might be useful. As an outlaw named Zeke Tolan he was useful. As Danny Spence he was just some unlucky ranch hand who'd got almost got himself hanged by mistake. 'Yeah,' he said. 'I'm Zeke Tolan.'

Abel laughed. 'Is that right?' he asked Spence. 'You're really Zeke Tolan after all? Why'd you tell me you weren't?'

'The sheriff might've been listening at the door,' said Spence, thinking quicker than he'd ever had to think in his life.

Ma studied him a little more, but she still kept the gun pointed at him, aimed right between his eyes. A

Colt .45 is a heavy piece of metal, but her arm just stayed rigid. 'If I let you ride with us, you going to do what I say, when I say it, no questions?'

'Yes, ma'am,' said Spence.

'You ain't going to cause me no trouble?'

'No, ma'am.'

'If you hesitate for one heartbeat to carry out one of my orders, that heartbeat will be your last. You understand me, boy?'

'Yes, ma'am.'

'Good,' she said.

Then she squeezed the trigger.

For a moment Spence thought he was dead. Then he realized he wasn't dead. He was still standing on the gallows with the Arizona sun baking his brain, his wrists tied behind his back, and the noose around his neck. But the rope was now hanging down his back.

Ma Cole had shot clean through it.

She shouted at Virgil, 'Cut his wrists free. We need to put some miles between us and this hole.'

'Stagecoach could be here soon,' said one of the horsemen.

'I don't give a wooden nickel for no stagecoach,' said Ma. 'It's the army I'm worried about. They got a fort about twenty miles away, and they send a patrol through these parts sometimes. You never know when they're gonna turn up.'

Virgil cut the rope that bound Spence's wrists. Spence pulled the noose from his neck.

Nothing in his life had ever felt so good as pulling away that noose.

Abel and Virgil ran down the gallows steps. Spence followed them. Virgil climbed up onto his horse, Abel clambered up behind him.

Spence said, 'Who do I ride with?'

Nobody offered to let him ride with them. Ma Cole looked around, pointed her gun down a side-street. 'There's a horse tethered down there,' she said. 'All saddled up and ready. Take it.'

For about one hundredth of a second Spence thought about saying he wouldn't do it. Stealing a horse would hang you as sure as murder. Even if the horse belonged to one of the townsfolk lying dead here at his feet, stealing a horse was stealing a horse. But the thought didn't last long, not with Ma watching him. So he took the horse.

He rode back to Ma and her gang, and when he reached them they set off out of town.

They were headed south.

They rode without another word for the next four hours. Ma Cole rode behind Spence most of the way, and all of the time she was behind him, Spence could feel her eyes upon him.

Two hundred miles south, over the border in a little town in Sonora, the real Zeke Tolan was drinking tequila.

His gang were with him. Two minutes earlier the taverna had been quiet, just the elderly Mexican fellow behind the bar, and another Mexican, drinking tequila in a corner. Then Zeke and his men had burst in, and they'd wanted the place to themselves, so they'd grabbed the Mexican in the corner and thrown him out into the street.

There wasn't any law in this town. There was supposed to be law here, a bunch of *federales*, but they were out in the hills shooting it out with some of Pancho Villa's revolutionaries. Which meant that right now the only law was what Zeke Tolan said it was.

'There ain't no *señoritas* in this town,' complained Tom Walker, after checking the back room to see if there were any women in there. Walker couldn't leave women alone. 'Where are all the *señoritas*?'

Jed Foley said, 'They most like heard you were coming, and hid.'

Walker went up to the elderly Mexican, grabbed his shirt and hauled him up so he was sprawled on top of his own bar. '*¿Dónde están todas las chicas?*' he demanded.

The elderly man said, '*No lo sé, señor.*'

'Yes you do,' said Walker, reverting to English. He kept hold of the elderly gentleman with one hand, and pulled out his gun with the other. He held the barrel to the man's head. 'Now tell me! And if you say, "I don't know" again, I'm liable to put a bullet in your brain!'

The man stared at him wide-eyed and jabbered incoherently, not knowing what to say.

'Useless goddamn Mexican!' snarled Walker. 'Be more use conversing with a rattlesnake.' He swiped the man across the head with the barrel of the revolver. The man slid off the bar and crumpled to the floor, out cold.

Zeke Tolan wasn't fussed about what his men did when they were between jobs, so long as they didn't question his authority. There was only one out of his nine men he was concerned about on that score, and that was Burt Murphy.

Tolan had seen the way Murphy had been acting lately, giving him sly looks when he thought Zeke wasn't looking, sulking and muttering. Tolan knew what all that meant. He could read the signs. He'd seen them before, in other men. Men who weren't around any more.

And right now, Murphy was in the same corner they'd dragged the Mexican out of, huddled together with young Sam Noone.

Well, don't they look like a pair of conspirators if ever I saw 'em, thought Tolan.

Tolan sat and waited till young Noone had to pay a visit to the latrine, and followed him out.

The latrine, such as it was, was behind the taverna. A wall without a roof, was all it was. Tolan waited a little more, till Noone had finished what he'd come out there to do, and when he came out from behind the wall, he said, 'How you doing, Sam?'

Noone was surprised to see Tolan. He was only seventeen, eighteen years old, something like that, and wasn't too good at hiding what he felt. You could read everything on his face, plain as words printed in a book.

'I – I'm just fine, sir,' said Noone, starting to blush already.

'I'm mighty glad to hear that,' said Tolan. 'I worry about you, my boy. I worry about you like you were my own kin. I've been looking out for you near two years now. You was just an orphan, nobody to care for you, when I told you you could ride with me – am I right?'

'That's – that's right, Mr Tolan,' said Noone, blinking rapidly, like he always did when he was scared.

'I told you to call me Zeke when it's just the two of us,' said Tolan. 'I think of you like my kid brother. Ain't right you should call me Mr Tolan. The others, they call me Mr Tolan, and maybe you should too when they're around, otherwise it could cause bad feeling. But when we're alone, you should call me Zeke.'

'Yes, sir. I mean, Zeke.'

'That's better.' Tolan got up closer to him. 'Now, I want you to come to me if anybody's been filling your head with crazy notions. I don't want you coming to no harm.'

'I – I sure appreciate that, Zeke,' stammered Noone.

'If anybody has been filling your head with crazy notions, I want to hear about it straight away, you understand me?'

'Sure, Zeke.'

Noone couldn't look Tolan in the eye.

'Has somebody been saying something to you, Sam?' asked Tolan. 'If there is, I promise I shan't be angry. Not at you.'

Noone gulped a couple of times, then he said, 'It's just . . .'

'What is it, Sam? Spit it out.'

'It's Murphy. He's been saying things.'

'What kind of things, Sam?'

'Well . . . I don't want to cause no trouble. . . .'

'You ain't going to cause no trouble, Sam. If there's trouble, it's on account of Murphy. Is he set on making trouble?'

'I guess.'

'How, exactly?'

Another couple of gulps and a flurry of rapid blinking. 'Well . . you know how they call you "Lucky Zeke", on account of you was always so lucky?'

'I'm aware of that. What about it?'

'Well, Murphy was saying as how maybe they shouldn't call you "Lucky" no more, what with the last few jobs not going so well. Like that railroad job when three of the gang got killed?'

'Mason and Tunney and Porter. A crying shame.'

'And then there was that time in Gila Creek, when you said the bank was easy pickings, but when it came to it they had a load more deputies and such than you thought, and we had to shoot our way out, and we killed all them people, and two more of the gang got killed. . . .'

33

'I recall. But these things happen every now and again. It goes with the job. You understand that, don't you, Sam?'

'Sure I do, Zeke. But Murphy, he said you'd say something like that. He said you have to expect a job turning bad once in a while, but he said it's happening all the time now, and that's why he reckons you shouldn't be called "Lucky" any more. He reckons you should be called "Unlucky Zeke".'

'He said that?'

'Yeah.'

'And what does he want to do about it?'

'He – he said as how we should have a vote, and pick ourselves a new leader.'

Tolan nodded. 'And what do you reckon to that, Sam? You reckon we should vote ourselves a new leader?'

Noone said, 'No, sir. I mean – no, Zeke. I reckon you've just had a run of bad luck, but it won't last, and then you'll go back to being lucky again. And I don't reckon we should vote ourselves a new leader, neither. I reckon we should stick with you, seeing as you've always seen us right.'

'That I have,' said Tolan. 'And did Murphy mention who he thought should be the new leader?'

Noone looked down at the dirt and said, 'He said he should nominate himself. That's the word he used – "nominate". It means . . .'

'I know what it means,' said Tolan. He placed his hand on Noone's shoulder, and the boy flinched. 'I

34

want to thank you for telling me this, Sam. Why, I feel more like a brother to you now than I ever did before. Do you feel that way, Sam?'

'Yes, Zeke,' said Noone.

CHAPTER FIVE

Tolan let Noone go back into the taverna first, waiting awhile before he went in himself. When he went in he saw that Noone wasn't sitting with Murphy, he was drinking and playing poker with some of the other fellows at a different table. Murphy was still seated at the table in the corner he'd been at before. He hadn't shifted an inch.

Tolan sat a distance away from Murphy and watched him out of the corner of his eye. Over the course of the next hour Murphy drank almost a whole bottle of tequila, all the while shooting glances at Tolan. Tolan didn't have to look at him to feel the hatred that was coming at him from the table over there in that corner.

Tolan thought, *Does he really think I don't know what he's doing, trying to turn the gang against me, one by one, so he can get to be leader himself?*

Tolan reckoned that trying to take over somebody else's gang made you about as big a sonofabitch as you could be. It just wasn't right. If you wanted your own gang, you went out and got yourself one.

But if you did set out to steal somebody's gang, you'd better do it discreetly. Quietly. And not let the fellow you're stealing it from know what you're doing. Otherwise you're not just a sonofabitch, you're a fool too. And being a sonofabitch and a fool wasn't a good combination. It could easily get you killed.

Among the many things that Zeke Tolan had observed about Murphy was that he couldn't hold his liquor worth a damn. And Tolan reckoned that any piece of information, however small, was likely to prove useful sometime or another.

The world outside the taverna's windows had turned black when Murphy finally got up from of his seat and weaved his way around the table. 'I'm going to find a bed,' he slurred to anybody who might happen to be listening. Nobody was. The rest of the gang were either playing cards or out in the night somewhere, trying to hunt out *señoritas.*

Murphy staggered from the taverna, out into the night.

Where does he think he's going? Is he going to try and find himself a rooming house? What's going on in that tequila-befuddled brain of his?

Tolan followed him out into the night.

The street was deserted. No sounds from any of the mud-brick houses. No light showed in any windows. Tolan guessed that many of the townsfolk had gone somewhere else to escape the fighting between the revolutionaries and the *federales*, and those who remained were lying low till the gang had left town.

At the far end of the street a starved-looking mongrel was killing a rat it had just caught, and taking its time about it. The mongrel gripped the rat in its jaws and shook it and tossed it around, dropping it onto the bone-dry dirt before getting a fresh grip on it and shaking it again. And all the time the rat made pitiful screeching, squealing noises.

Between Tolan and the mongrel was Murphy, staggering around like the fool he was. Murphy stopped outside an adobe, stared at it for a second or two, then lurched forward and hammered on the door with his fist. 'Hey, let me in!' in shouted. 'I need a bed for the night! You hear me? Let me in!'

'Hey,' called Tolan, softly. 'What you doing, Murph?'

Murphy stopped hammering on the door and turned. He swayed a little, peering into the darkness. The moon was full and big and high, and cast deep shadows across the road. Tolan stood in one of the shadows, invisible.

'Who – who's that?' slurred Murphy.

Tolan stepped into the moonlight. 'It's me, Murph.'

Murphy stared. 'Oh – it's you, Mr Tolan. I didn't see you.'

Even though he was trying his best to play respectful, with his '*Mr Tolan*' and all, Tolan could see the hatred in Murphy's eyes.

'What you doing, Murph?' asked Tolan again.

38

'There might be decent, hard-working folk in there, trying to get some sleep. And there you go, trying to wake them up. Why don't you find yourself a rooming house?'

Murphy took a few seconds to get a grip on what Tolan was saying. 'I – I don't rightly know if there is a rooming house, Mr Tolan,' he said, swaying in the moonlight.

Behind him, at the far end of the street, the mongrel was still shaking the rat, shaking it, tossing it around, crushing it between its jagged teeth. The rat gave a piercing shriek, louder than before, then the shriek got cut short.

Murphy heard it. He turned around, nearly losing his footing and toppling over, but not quite. 'Wha – what was that?'

'A rat just got it neck broke,' said Zeke Tolan. 'Nothing to cry about. Ain't nobody in the world going to cry about a rat that gets its neck broke.'

Murphy watched the mongrel worrying at the rat's corpse, one of its front paws pinning down the body as it tried to pull away the head and expose the meat.

'I – I ain't crying about no rat,' he said.

'What?' snapped Tolan.

Murphy swayed some more. 'I said – I said I ain't crying, Mr Tolan.'

Tolan stepped forward a couple of paces. He estimated there was about twenty feet between them now. 'What the hell you jabbering about, Murph?' he snapped.

Murphy wiped his sleeve across his mouth. 'I'm – I'm talking about the rat,' he said.

'What rat?' demanded Tolan.

Murphy turned, pointed down the road. The mongrel had succeeded in pulling the rat's head off, and was now gnawing at the flesh while still keeping the body pinned with its front paw.

Tolan could see the blood pooling on the baked dirt, black in the moonlight, and darkening the mongrel's snout.

'That rat,' slurred Murphy.

'Goddamn it, Murph,' said Tolan, his voice rising. 'If you ain't the biggest fool I've ever met. What you doing, standing in the moonlight, yammerin' about rats? Is that any way for a grown man to behave?'

Murphy looked confused. He said, 'But you . . . you. . . .'

'I *what*?' asked Tolan.

'You were the one who. . . .'

'*What*?'

Murphy didn't know what to say. Maybe he was wondering if he'd dreamed Tolan saying nobody cried about a rat getting its neck broke. Murphy looked like he wasn't too sure about anything any more.

'I said, what the hell you talking about, Murph?' said Tolan, his voice rising. 'Are you some kind of a fool, yammerin' about rats and suchlike? Are you losing your goddamn mind?'

Murphy just stood there, swaying, looking at his feet.

'Look at me, goddamn it!' yelled Tolan.

Murph looked at him.

'You're a goddamn fool,' said Tolan. 'I should have left you where I found you. When you begged me to let you join the gang, I should've left you crawling around in the dirt. You're no more use than a goddamn worm!'

Murphy was getting riled. 'I – I never begged you!' He pulled his shoulders back so he was standing straight, all six foot three of him. 'And I ain't no worm, neither!'

'You're a worm,' said Tolan, saying it slow so that Murphy understood every word. 'Your pa was a worm, and as for your ma . . . I can't even guess what your ma was. . . .'

Murphy was a quick draw when he was sober. But Tolan was betting his life that Murphy wasn't so fast a draw when he had a bottle of tequila inside him, slowing him down, numbing his brain. He was a good shot too, but like everybody his accuracy suffered with distance. Every gunfight Tolan had witnessed between Murphy and anybody else – and Tolan had seen a few – Murphy and his opponent had been close, fifteen feet away, no more. So Tolan was hoping he'd judged the distance – twenty feet, more or less – about right. Tolan reckoned he could draw quick and hit Murphy in the belly or the chest at this distance, no problem. And hopefully he'd be quicker and more accurate than a drunk Murphy.

'Take that back,' said Murphy, not slurring so much

41

now. 'You take that back, you sonofabitch!'

'That's *Mr Tolan* to you, you goddamn worm,' said Tolan.

'Sonofabitch,' said Murphy.

Murphy went for his gun.

Like Tolan had thought, the tequila had slowed Murphy down. Not by much, but just enough so that Tolan fired the same time as Murphy. And the tequila had messed with Murphy's aim, too. His bullet zinged a foot or more past Tolan's left shoulder and hissed off into the night. Tolan's bullet hit Murphy square in the gut.

Murphy doubled over. Somehow he kept on his feet, though he staggered around some. And he kept hold of his gun. He tried to straighten up. He looked Tolan and raised his gun to fire again.

Tolan's second bullet hit Murphy in the chest. It knocked him backwards, and the next thing he was lying in the dirt, staring up at the stars in that big Mexican sky, the life oozing out of him.

Tolan went up to him, kicked the gun out of Murphy's hand. Murphy wasn't moving, but Tolan fired a bullet into his head, just to make sure.

By now the gang who were in the taverna were pouring out into the moonlight to see what was going on, including young Sam Noone. Jed Foley said, 'What happened?'

They were all looking at Zeke Tolan, then down at Murphy, then back at Tolan again.

'Murphy drew on me,' said Tolan. 'He wanted to

take over the gang. I couldn't let him do that. It's my gang, and that's how it's going to stay.' He spat on Murphy's lifeless body. Then he looked up at the gang. 'I killed him fair and square. Now get some sleep. We've got a hard day's riding tomorrow.'

Danny Spence rode with the Cole gang all the way down to their hideout, deep inside a canyon near the Mexican border. They had a mudbrick house in there, well hidden. You couldn't see it from outside the canyon.

Some of the Cole boys had wives, or at least women they treated as wives. One of the women was called Mercy, and she was Virgil Cole's woman.

There are some people who seem to be put on this earth just to cause trouble and heartbreak, and Mercy – as Spence was about to find out – was one of them.

CHAPTER SIX

The sun was going down by the time they'd unsaddled and fed the horses, so Ma Cole said, 'We all gotta get some sleep now. That's an order.'

They went inside the house, a one-floor adobe, long and low. There were only three rooms: the kitchen at one end, a room with a bed in it at the other end, and in the middle one long, low room with blankets scattered around.

Abel Cole found a blanket, threw it at Spence. 'That's yours,' said Abel.

'Where do I sleep?' asked Spence.

'On the floor, like the rest of us,' said Abel.

Spence looked around. Sure enough, everybody was kicking off their boots and stretching themselves out on the floor under a blanket, including the couples.

'Who sleeps in the bedroom? Ma?' he asked.

'Nobody sleeps in the bedroom,' said Abel. 'If

anybody needs privacy, they go in there.'

Nobody was using the bedroom tonight.

'Where's the latrine?' asked Spence, sitting on the floor next to Abel, pulling off his boots, laying flat and covering himself with the blanket.

'You go outside,' said Abel. 'Around back. There's bushes there. If you want to wash, there's a spring, and a pool.'

Spence noticed Ma wasn't sleeping on the floor. She was spread out on a long wooden box, her blanket over her, already snoring. 'Why's your ma sleeping on a box?' he whispered.

'That's a coffin,' said Abel. 'My pa's inside it.'

'Your pa? You mean there's a dead body in there?'

Abel giggled softly. Whispered, 'Well, he ain't going to be in there *alive*, is he?'

Spence wasn't sure anything would surprise him. 'But don't it . . . I mean. . . . Don't take this wrong, but what about the smell?'

'He's mummified,' said Abel. 'Like those redskins they have outside stores.'

Spence knew what mummified meant, more or less, but he'd never seen any mummified redskins outside stores.

Abel said, 'Ain't you ever seen a mummified redskin standing outside a store, standing there, like he's alive, with a headdress and everything?'

'No,' said Spence. 'I never had. But I spent most of my time on ranches.' He wasn't sure he ever wanted to see a mummified redskin, either. It didn't seem right to do that to a person after they were dead, whether they were a redskin or whoever they were, mummify them and prop them up outside a store like they were alive. 'Why'd they do that? Dress them and stand them outside stores like that?'

'Folk come from miles around to see it, then they go into the store and buy stuff. Why do you think?'

Spence could see how that would work, but that didn't make it right.

'Ma loved Pa so much, she couldn't bear to be parted from him,' whispered Abel. 'She wouldn't let anybody else do it. Took out some of his innards, and replaced them with sand, then lay him in the sun till he dried out. She sat there in her rocking chair with a rifle to stop birds and critters getting at him, then she bound him up, put him in the box and she's been sleeping on top of him ever since. Says she can't get a wink of sleep unless she'd laying on top of her beloved Hector.'

Spence lay in the darkness, listening to the snoring all around him, doubting if he'd be able to get any sleep at all.

But he must have gone to sleep, because the next thing he knew sunlight was coming in through the windows, and then Ma Cole kicked his foot and said, 'Time to get up.'

'Tomorrow we ride for Paradise Flats,' said Ma. 'There's a bank there, got a load of ranchers' money in it. It's four days' ride from here, so you all need to

46

get some rest.'

So the men all rested. There were eight men in all, five of them Ma's sons: Abel, who was the youngest; Virgil, Dwight, Edwin and Hector Junior, who was the eldest. Then there were the other gang members who Ma had picked up along the way, one way or another: Tom Bradley, Jack O'Brien and Danny Spence himself. And then there were the women. Four of them, not counting Ma. The four eldest Cole boys had women.

It was Mercy, Virgil's 'wife', who caused the trouble.

The women swept the place, kept it clean, and did the cooking.

It was the middle of the afternoon when Spence went down to the spring to wash.

The spring was about a quarter of a mile south-east of the house, secluded, shielded from the house by rocks and scrub and tall saguaro cactuses, some of them thirty, forty feet high.

Abel had told him where the spring was, so Spence went down there, stripped off the dust-caked clothes he'd been wearing the last three weeks, and then peered down into the pool, wondering if there were any critters in there. Abel had told him it was safe, but Spence believed in checking things for himself, on account he reckoned that was the only way you could be sure about anything.

He couldn't see any critters so he rinsed out his clothes and lay them out flat on the rocks to dry in the fierce desert sun. Then he lowered himself into the cool water and scraped the grime off his skin.

When he'd got about as much off as he could, he lay down next to the pool, with his head in the shadow of a saguaro, and waited for his body to dry.

Spence wasn't a fool. His six-gun lay in another patch of shade within inches of his right hand.

He wondered how he was going to get himself out of this situation. He reckoned that being stuck with the Cole gang, all of them at least half crazy so far as he could tell, was in its way nearly as dangerous as being locked in that Gila Creek jail, waiting to hang.

He pondered the matter a short while, and came to the conclusion that there wasn't much he could do about it right now. If he took off on his own, on one of the horses, Ma would most like track him down, and wouldn't rest till she'd killed him. Or till he'd killed her. And if he killed her, then her sons wouldn't rest till they had his head on a stick. Not that he could steal a horse anyway – they were all in a big cave within sight of the house, along with the Gatling gun and the rest of the Cole's equipment, with the gang taking turns standing guard.

Spence decided he'd have to wait and see what providence had in store, and if an opportunity arose to get out clean, he'd take it. Till then there was no use fretting over it, so he forced his mind to stop chasing its own tail needlessly, and started to doze.

He'd been dozing for a few minutes when a hand clamped over his mouth.

Spence made a grab for his gun, but it wasn't there.

He sprang to his feet, and found himself looking down the barrel of his own six-gun.

CHAPTER SEVEN

It was Mercy, Virgil's woman.

She was naked as the day she was born, her dress folded up neatly and placed on a rock some yards away. On top of the folded dress was the grubby pink ribbon she used to tied up her hair. Without the ribbon, her yellow hair hung lank and greasy down to her waist.

She was no more than about twenty years old, something like that. About five feet tall in her bare feet, and so thin her bones stuck out. She was wiry, though. Hard work had toughened her up. He could see her muscles working beneath the skin. Her breasts were small but rounded. Spence reckoned she might have been pretty once, but her face had become lined already, with deep creases around her mouth and brown smudges under her eyes. She grinned at him as she pointed the gun at his chest. Her teeth were yellow, and a couple of them were missing. She put a finger to her lips, which were about her best feature, full and ripe. '*Shhh. . .* Don't make any sound, or Ma will hear us.'

She was worried about Ma, Spence noticed. Not Virgil, her man, or any of the others. Just Ma.

Spence's first inclination was to ask what she wanted, but he realized how foolish that question would be, so instead he said, 'Put the gun down.'

She didn't. She kept it pointed at his chest. A heavy gun for a five-foot-nothing woman, barely more than a girl, but the weight of it didn't seem to bother her.

'Lie down,' she said.

'If you want what I reckon you want, you've sure got a funny way of asking for it,' he told her.

She giggled, and Spence saw her finger tighten on the trigger. 'I ain't asking,' she said. 'I'm tellin'. Now get on your back.'

Everybody here is just plum loco, he thought. Any other occasion, he might have been tempted. He had the same urges as any other man. But if there was one thing that was guaranteed to kill those urges stone dead, pointing a loaded gun at him was it. And having a crazy woman and her crazy sons only a couple of hundred yards away – one of them this woman's so-called husband – didn't help much.

'I said, *get on your back!*'

He sat on the rock and lay down. 'You know, we could get better acquainted if you put that gun down,' he said.

'We do it my way. All my life I got to do things the way somebody else says. Well, now I get to do things my way, because I got the gun. . . .' She took a step closer, her bare feet padding on the rock.

'Any second, somebody could come along and see us,' he said. 'Then what? Ma would skin us both alive.'

'I don't care,' she said. She was standing over him now, her legs either side of him, pointing the gun at his face.

'I'd be a mite more enthusiastic if you stopped pointing that at me,' he said.

'You let me worry about that,' she told him. 'Anyway, you don't know exactly what I got in mind yet.'

A second or two later, Spence was just getting an idea of what she had in mind when a voice shouted, 'Mercy! You goddamn whore! I see you!'

It was one of the other women who'd seen them. It turned out her name was Edith, a tall, gaunt, raven-haired woman with an accent that sounded like it came from way over Louisiana way, or someplace like that.

Edith started hollering, shouting for Ma and the rest of them.

Mercy threw the gun into the pool. Why she did that, Spence could only guess. Maybe in a panic she thought that if it was out of sight under the water, she could deny she'd ever been holding it, or something. Not that that made any sense. But people do things when they're panicked that make no sense, and can't really account for them later.

Spence heard the splash of the gun entering the water, got up and went into the water after it.

Mercy ran to where she'd left her dress, pulled it over her head and started tying her hair up with that dirty pink ribbon.

She'd just about finished tying the ribbon when Ma and the rest of them turned up. 'He was trying to rape me, Ma!' she yelled.

'That's bull,' shouted Edith. 'She was pointing a gun at him and about to make him . . .'

'That's a lie!' screamed Mercy. 'I don't have no gun!'

'She threw it in the pool,' said Edith.

'I did not!' yelled Mercy.

By now Spence had found the gun. He lifted it clear of the water. 'I sure as hell didn't throw my own gun in the pool,' he said, climbing out onto the rocks.

Ma screamed at Mercy, 'I always knew you was a whore! I told Virgil you was a whore when he brought you here, but he didn't listen. So long as you behaved yourself I was willing to let things be, but I knew there'd come a day when something like this would happen.'

Virgil had been standing next to Ma all this time, his face all the time getting redder and angrier. 'I'll kill you!' he yelled, running at Spence.

Virgil threw a punch at Spence, but Spence dodged the blow and hit Virgil with a right cross that knocked him on his ass.

Virgil shook his head to clear his brain and sprang

back up onto his feet. He looked like he was going to try his luck with Spence again, but Ma fired her gun in the air to put a stop to the fighting and shouted at Virgil: 'Haven't you heard a word that's been said? Your woman was holding a gun on him! Besides, we need an extra man after Wilson got himself killed.'

Spence hadn't heard mention of any Wilson, and never heard another word about him after that.

'But he was . . .' began Virgil.

'He was doing nothing,' said Ma. 'This is all your whore's doing, nobody else's. Now get back over here!'

Virgil obediently went back to where he was standing before, next to Ma.

'*You!*' Ma yelled at Spence. 'Get dressed!'

Spence pulled on his clothes.

'What you going to do with her?' asked Edith, glaring at Mercy.

Spence kind of got the impression that Edith and Mercy weren't too fond of one another.

Ma turned to Virgil. 'You still want her, even though you know she's a whore?'

Virgil looked down at his feet. 'I don't rightly know,' he mumbled.

'Either you do or you don't,' said Ma. 'If you want to keep her, then keep her. But if you do, you'll know that anytime your back's turned, she'll be whoring around with any man she can find. We'd better mess up her face some, so no other man will want her.'

'But she's so pretty,' said Virgil.

'Used to be,' said Ma. 'Not so much now. So which is it to be? You can keep her, with her face messed up, or we get rid of her.'

Virgil didn't know what to say. He just kept looking down at his feet, his face red. Spence thought he might have been crying.

Ma put her arm around his shoulder and pulled him to her.

'I don't know what to do, Ma,' he said.

'It's all right, Virgil. Ma will make everything all right again. Best thing we can do for you is find you another woman. One that ain't a whore. Ma will find you one after we rob the bank in Paradise Flats. Would you like that?'

Virgil gave a little nod.

'It's for the best,' said Ma. She pointed the gun at Mercy, who was still standing there by the side of the pool, and shot Mercy twice, once in the gut and once in the head.

Mercy crumpled onto the rock.

Ma, still comforting Virgil, said to a couple of her other sons, 'Put her out in the desert. No need to bury her. Just strip her, bring her dress and that ribbon back here and burn 'em. The coyotes and the vultures can take care of her.'

Virgil nodded at Spence, glared at him with wet, hate-filled eyes. 'What about him?'

Ma looked at Spence. 'Throw your gun over here,' she said, pointing her gun at him.

Spence hesitated. But a moment later there were

five or six guns pointed at him, so he threw the gun over in Ma's direction, and one of her boys scooped it up.

Ma whispered something in Virgil's ear. Whatever it was, it calmed Virgil down some. 'OK, Ma,' he said.

Everybody went back to the house, except for the two sons who'd been given the job of hauling Mercy's body out into the desert. Soon they'd gone too, and Spence was on his own again, wondering what Ma had said to Virgil.

Paradise Flats was getting to be quite a town. Nowhere near as big as Tucson, but on its way. The railway passed through, and the railroad had brought building materials and people, and money. It had brick buildings, some of them three stories high, and there was talk of gas lighting on Main Street, though nobody seriously thought that would happen for a while yet.

It had three banks, and one of these was the Cattle Ranchers' Mutual, on the corner of Freemont Street and Main. The Mutual was the largest, and had a big safe in the manager's office full of ranchers' money.

A gang had tried to rob it four months earlier. They'd gone in with guns and shot some customers, and shot a teller, but they hadn't been able to get to the money because of the steel bars and the steel door that separated the front of the bank from the rear, where the money was. They'd left empty-handed, and the moment they'd run out into the street they'd been gunned down by the sheriff and five of his deputies.

They had a whole load of deputies in Paradise Flats.

The gang hadn't known about the steel bars and the steel doors. They just hadn't done any research. They were used to old-fashioned banks where you could just leap over the divide between the customers and tellers and hold a gun to the manager's head while he opened the safe.

But Ma Cole had done her research. She always did her research. She knew every square inch of that bank, and knew exactly how it should be robbed.

She knew about all those steel bars, and she'd heard that the manager wasn't an easy man to threaten. Hold a gun to his head, he'd like as not tell you to go to hell.

The gang all wore long grey duster coats, despite the harsh afternoon sun, so they knew who was in the gang and who wasn't. And with their Boss of the Plains hats pulled down low, and bandannas over their faces, it would be impossible for anybody to identify them.

Before they entered town, Ma said, 'Remember the golden rule: nobody says anybody's name. If you call anybody by name, I'll whip you till you're damn near dead, I don't care who you are.'

Nobody looked at the gang twice as they rode down Main Street, with their bandannas covering their mouths and noses. Main Street hadn't got itself paved yet, it was still hard-packed dirt, and plumes of dust rose every time a horse's hoof thudded down on it. So wearing a bandanna over your face wasn't suspicious, it was practical, a lot of riders did it. It was either that or get your lungs full of dust.

Hector Junior followed on behind, driving the wagon that carried the Gatling gun, covered by a tarpaulin. Edwin sat at his side, cradling a Springfield on his lap.

Two of the gang had peeled off at the edge of town, and were now busy elsewhere.

As they approached the bank, Ma reached inside her duster and pulled out a large turnip pocket watch. She studied it as the hands crept closer to three o'clock.

When it got to three, an explosion boomed out as two sticks of dynamite ripped apart the back of the sheriff's office, two hundred yards down Freemont Street.

People started screaming.

Ma watched as deputies ran out of the sheriff's office, onto the street.

Then a second explosion boomed: another two sticks of dynamite, but these had been placed inside a barrel full of nails.

The nails tore like bullets through the people trying to escape the sheriff's office, and through any other townsfolk who happened to be passing by.

Spence hadn't known that was going to happen. He'd known they were going to rob a bank, and that there'd be a signal, but Ma hadn't said what the signal would be. Now he felt sick in his gut as he watched the carnage. Not that he could do much about it. They still hadn't given him his gun back, and they'd been watching him closely all the way from their hideout.

Ma returned the watch to her pocket, and pulled out a tin whistle. She blew on it once, hard.

That was their signal to go in.

Ma prodded Spence with her gun. 'Get off your horse. We're going in.'

Spence and Ma and two of her sons dismounted, and handed the reins to Virgil, who remained on his horse. That was his job: to keep hold of the horses.

Meanwhile, Edwin pulled the tarp away from the Gatling gun and started firing. The wagon was positioned at the centre of the junction between Main Street and Freemont Street, so he could fire in any direction. He fired a short burst back the way they'd come, then up and down the dissecting road. Then he paused, letting the gun cool, but all the time swinging around, watching for any deputies, or any other fool who wanted to try being heroic.

Spence hadn't been told the whole story, just that he had to go in there and stick close to Ma.

As they were about to enter the bank, Ma hissed to Spence, 'One false move, I'll shoot you. And I'll shoot you so you'll bleed out slow.'

They went in, Abel and Dwight first, then Spence, with Ma behind him.

The first thing Abel and Dwight did was, they shot a customer each, both of them shouting, 'Get down on the floor, you sons of bitches! And get your hands above your heads!

Spence had heard about bank raids where the

robbers went in and shot at the ceiling or the floor as a warning. He'd never heard of anybody shooting people as they went in. But he figured that the Coles had killed so many people that a few more didn't matter.

Dwight stayed by the door to stop anybody getting out, and stop anybody getting in.

Outside on the street there was screaming, but it was far off. Spence reckoned most of the townspeople didn't know what was happening. They didn't know the bank was being robbed. There'd been the two explosions, and then the rattle of the Gatling gun. They were scared and confused.

But it was only going to be a matter of time before somebody figured it out.

Ma prodded Spence in the back with her six-gun. 'Move,' she ordered.

She pushed him towards one end of the row of cashiers' booths. Spence thought that was mighty strange, because the steel door that led through to the business side of the bank was at the other end of the row.

'Get on the floor, face down, and don't move,' she said.

Spence got on the floor of the lobby. It was cool stone, smooth. He had no idea why she'd made him lie down. One of the customers lying close by, a fat rancher with a big white moustache, was confused too. He looked at Spence oddly, wondering why this fellow who was dressed like the other robbers – grey duster coat, bandanna, King of the Plains hat pulled down – was being treated the same as the customers.

There was another burst from the Gatling gun, and more screaming from far off down the street.

A few more seconds passed, then Ma blew on her tin whistle again, and the next thing she was laying down flat beside him.

He looked at her.

'Cover your head,' she muttered.

Spence covered his head.

There was a bang, and a noise of tearing metal. He felt the heat of the blast even through the fabric of the duster. A chunk of steel hit the wall above his head.

There was a second or two of silence, then somebody started whimpering, and somebody else started screaming.

Spence felt a kick in his side. Ma was on her feet again. 'Get up,' she said.

He got up and she said, 'Through the door. Quick. We ain't on no picnic.'

The steel door had been blasted open, buckled in the middle where the locking mechanism had been. The door hung open. It had been torn away from the bottom hinge, but the top one held, just.

They went through the door, into the area behind the cashiers' booths. The cashiers who'd been closest to the door were dead. There was a lot of blood, and a smell like you get when you brand a steer. Spence didn't want to look around him too much. He kept his eyes ahead.

The next door was just a regular wood panel door, and that also had been blasted open by the explosion. Beyond it was a white-painted corridor, maybe twenty feet from one end to the other, two doors on either side and another door at the end.

The door at the end had 'Manager' painted in gold leaf on the frosted glass panel set into the upper half. Spence thought it was kind of funny how the glass hadn't shattered, but it hadn't, and that's all there was to it.

'Get on the floor,' said Ma.

Spence was getting a little sick of people telling him to do this and do that. Lie on the floor, throw away your gun, steal that horse, whatever else. He'd managed to get through his whole life so far without killing a single soul, but he reckoned it wouldn't be too long before he'd have to. And till now it had never crossed his mind he might one day have to kill a woman.

He got on the floor again, wishing that she'd let her guard drop for a fraction of a second so he could grab one of the guns she was holding.

Ma knelt on one knee and fired a bullet through the glass pane with 'Manager' on it, then she ducked. And a moment after she'd ducked, somebody from inside the office fired out, twice, the bullets hissing over their heads.

A man shouted from the office: 'I'm the manager of this here bank, and while there's a breath in my body, I ain't gonna let you steal one cent of my customers' money!'

'Suits me fine,' said Ma. She put away her six-guns and from deep inside her duster coat she pulled out a sawn-off double-barrelled shotgun that Spence figured she must have been carrying in some kind of holster.

The shotgun had been sawed at both ends, the butt cut down so there was barely enough of it left to grip. She held it like a pistol, one-handed, and aimed it at the door. Not the glass panel, but the wooden lower half of the door.

She squeezed the right-hand trigger and the gun boomed. Holding it the way she was, the recoil would have been enough to dislocate most men's shoulder, but Ma was strong; the recoil didn't bother her at all.

The shotgun wasn't loaded with regular cartridges full of pellets. These cartridges held only one steel ball bearing, big as a thumbnail.

The steel ball punched through the door, leaving a hole in the wood the size of a fist.

'What you say now, bank manager?' asked Ma.

The bank manager didn't reply.

Ma returned the sawn-off to the holster under her coat, and again pulled out her six-gun. She ran to the door and kicked it open.

Whatever else Ma Cole is, Spence thought, *she's brave.* He couldn't think of more than three men he'd ever met who would have done that: run to the door and kick it open, not knowing if the fellow on the other side was dead or not.

Ma turned her head, said to Spence, 'Get up. Come in here.'

So he did just that, and when he got inside the office he saw the bank manager lying on the floor, and there wasn't much left of the man's face.

'There's the safe,' said Ma. 'Open it!'

The safe door was about the size of a regular door, painted green and made of steel, and the safe itself was big enough for a man to step into and walk around. Big enough for thousands of US Dollars in banknotes, maybe some gold and a lot more else besides.

It wasn't the kind of safe door that opened with a key. It was the kind with a combination lock, a dial with numbers all around. Mr Buchanan, owner of the Lazy Q ranch, had a safe with a combination lock – Spence had seen it once – though Mr Buchanan's was a lot smaller than this one.

Spence stared at the dial with the numbers all around, knowing there wasn't a chance in hell he'd be able to open it.

Ma Cole saw him staring at the safe and said, 'Well, what you waiting for? Why'd you think I brought you along? Everybody knows Zeke Tolan is the best safe-cracker this side of the Missouri. Now get that goddamn safe open! We don't have a whole heap of time to waste.'

CHAPTER EIGHT

Spence had heard a lot about what a murdering sonof-abitch Zeke Tolan was supposed to be, but nobody had said anything about him being a safe cracker, till now.

It came as something of a surprise.

He realized what it must have been that Ma had whispered to Virgil down at the pool. Something like: '*We need him to open the safe, but soon as he's done that, I'll kill him.*' Something like that.

Spence had read quite a bit in his time, by lamp-light in the bunkhouse of an evening. Magazines, like old copies of *The Atlantic Monthly*, and books and so forth. There wasn't a lot else to do on a ranch at night. Some of the stories had told how thieves broke into rich people's houses and opened safes full of jewellery.

The thieves would sometimes use doctors' stetho-scopes to listen out for the 'tumblers'. Spence knew that these 'tumblers' had something to do with the locking mechanism, and you could hear them doing something or other – tumbling, he guessed – when you turned the dial. But that was about all he knew.

He didn't have a stethoscope, and Ma Cole was watching him close, likely starting to wonder why he was staring at the safe instead of trying to open it. So he knelt in front of the safe and pressed his ear against the green-painted metal.

He turned the dial clockwise, real slow.

Spence listened hard for something that sounded like a tumbler tumbling, whatever, but he was damned if he could hear anything.

As he turned the dial he noticed that the dead bank manager's right hand was about three feet from his knee.

And in the dead bank manager's right hand was a big old .44 calibre Smith & Wesson 'Russian'.

Spence carried on turning the dial. He gave a satisfied grunt, as if he'd heard the mechanism do something he approved of, and started turning the dial the other way.

There was another rattle from the Gatling gun out on the street. Spence said to Ma, 'Tell that boy of yours to quit firing that Gatling gun a minute, will you? I can't hear the tumblers, what with him making all that noise.'

He must have sounded like he knew what he was talking about, because Ma made about the first mistake she'd made since he'd met her. She turned and started heading for the door.

Spence grabbed the Smith & Wesson from out of

the dead man's fingers at about the same moment Ma realized she'd done something dumb.

Deputy Joe Pooley was settling some trouble at the Ol' Mississippi saloon over on North Street when he heard the explosions. He was on foot, so he started running towards Main Street, and he hadn't gone far before he heard the rattle of the Gatling gun.

Whatever was happening, it was something big. A bank robbery, had to be. Probably the Cattle Ranchers' Mutual, as that was the biggest prize.

Pooley had once heard somebody say it'd take an army to rob the Cattle Ranchers' Mutual. Well, it looked like somebody had got themselves one.

He'd got to the junction of Higgs Street and Main when another deputy, a man named Wynne, saw him and said, 'They've blown up the sheriff's office. I heard the sheriff was killed!'

Joe Pooley heard the words, but it took a second or two before he could make sense of them. He'd thought the sheriff was about the closest thing a person could be to indestructible.

'A gang's robbing the Cattle Rancher's Mutual,' continued Wynne. 'They blew up the telegraph office, too. They got a Gatling gun on a wagon at the junction of Freemont and Main, and they're shooting anybody who gets close.'

Freemont Street was three blocks down from where they were standing.

Pooley edged to the corner of the building and

peered around. Sure enough, he could see the Gatling gun mounted on the wagon, some two hundred yards away.

'How many deputies still alive that you know about?' asked Joe.

'I only seen you and Matt Culpepper.'

'Where's Matt?'

'Gone to get his best rifle from home. He should be back any minute. He reckons he can stay out of the range of that Gatling gun and still get an accurate shot at the sonofabitch who's firing it.'

The Gatling gun chattered again, and this time it was in their direction. There wasn't anybody on Freemont or Main, now. Nobody alive, anyway. The fellow operating the Gatling was firing short bursts in each direction in turn, to dissuade anybody from interfering with the bank robbery.

The windows of a rooming house cater-corner from where they were standing shattered.

'You were in the army,' Pooley said to Wynne. 'You know much about Gatlings?'

'I'd say that sounds like a .30 calibre, not a .58 calibre,' said Wynne. 'That means it can fire at a rate of 400 to 900 rounds per minute.'

'What else you know?'

'They're not accurate at more than about one hundred feet, but they don't have to be. Not when it fires over 400 bullets in a single minute. You fire in the general direction of your intended target and move the gun around some, pretty soon you're liable to hit it.'

Just now Culpepper turned up with his best rifle. Like Wynne, Culpepper had also served time in the army, except that whereas Wynne had been an expert horseman, Culpepper had been an expert marksman. In the army he'd used a Krag-Jorgensen, which had been chosen as the standard rifle of the US Army, and this had been his weapon of choice ever since.

Culpepper had once told Pooley he could hit a silver dollar at a range of six thousand feet with this rifle, though Pooley had no idea if that was just bragging.

'Can you hit the sonofabitch with the Gatling from here?' asked Pooley.

'Sure I can,' said Culpepper.

'Do it, then.'

Culpepper knelt at the corner of the building and aimed the long barrel down Main Street.

'Sonofabitch has seen me,' said Culpepper.

The Gatling gun chattered. Bullets zinged through the air above Culpepper's head.

Culpepper fired only once, but that was enough.

The Gatling stopped chattering.

'You get him?' asked Pooley.

'I got him,' said Culpepper. 'Now let me see if I can't hit the other fellow, the one with him. . . . He's looking around, trying to figure out where the shot came from. . . . He's seen me. . . .'

Culpepper fired again.

'Well?' asked Pooley.

'Got him in the brain,' said Culpepper. 'Now let's

see if anybody pokes their head out of that there bank. . . . Yup. Here's somebody, dressed just the same as the other two, with the duster coat and everything. . . .'

Culpepper fired a third time.

'Damn!' said Culpepper.

'What's up?' asked Wynne. 'You miss him?'

'No, I did not miss him,' said Culpepper, sounding a mite offended.

'What, then?'

'I was aiming between his eyes,' said Culpepper. 'Instead I shot him in the mouth.'

'Is he dead?' asked Wynne.

'If he ain't, he soon will be,' said Culpepper.

'So what you complaining about?' asked Pooley.

'I ain't complaining,' said Culpepper. 'I just like to hit what I aim at, that's all.'

CHAPTER NINE

Even as Ma Cole spun around, Spence knew he couldn't kill her. She was a woman, after all. And somehow, despite her being a killer and about the lowest form of life he'd ever met, he still couldn't do it.

He shot her in the leg with the bank manager's Smith & Wesson, the bullet shattering her right thigh bone. It knocked her clean off her feet. She crashed to the floor, dropping the gun she was holding as she clutched at her injured leg.

Spence got up, grabbed her six-gun and relieved her of the sawn-off, threw them down the corridor, and ran towards the front of the bank.

'You sonofabitch!' yelled Ma, once she'd found her voice again. 'I'll get you, you bastard!'

In the lobby, the customers were still lying on their bellies, their arms covering their heads.

Abel had stayed in the lobby, along with Dwight. Dwight had been guarding the door, and Abel had been watching the customers and the bank tellers, making sure none of them got any smart ideas.

Spence had been expecting to have to shoot them, but when he got to the lobby he saw Abel standing in the middle of the room, his hands down by his sides, staring at Dwight.

Dwight had been shot. He lay on his back, half-in and half-out of the doorway. There was a hole in the bandanna tied across his face, and a pool of blood was spreading across the floor under his head.

'They shot Dwight,' said Abel, as if he didn't really believe it. 'They shot him in the mouth. He's dead.'

Ma was still screaming, her shrill voice echoing down the corridor from the bank manager's office. Abel heard her, and came out of his trance. He looked at Spence. 'What happened to Ma?' Then he realized that Spence shouldn't be out here in the lobby, not without Ma, and he saw the wisp of smoke curling out of the barrel of the Smith & Wesson Spence held.

Abel raised his gun to shoot Spence, but Spence got him first, a bullet to the gut.

Abel doubled over, but still he tried to aim his gun at Spence, so Spence had to shoot him again, and this time the bullet went into his heart, and he crashed to the floor stone dead.

Spence looked at Abel lying on the floor, the first man he'd ever killed. He hadn't even shot a man before. He stood there for a moment, thinking about that. But then he reckoned he would have to stop thinking about it. He wasn't in the clear yet. So far as the good people of Paradise Flats were concerned, he was just another member of the gang that had killed a load of people while trying to rob a bank, and it wouldn't do any good trying to tell them he'd been forced into it. They wouldn't listen any more than the folk in Gila Creek had listened when he'd told them he wasn't Zeke Tolan.

Spence tore off the duster coat and threw away the hat. He kept the bandanna around his face. He didn't want any of the customers lying on the floor to be able to recognize him later, regardless of whether they mistook him for that Zeke Tolan fellow. A brown derby hat lay at his feet, its dome of a crown dented on one side. He put it on his head, shoved the Smith & Wesson into his waistband and ran out of the door.

Virgil, who'd been taking care of the horses, was nowhere to be seen, and the horses had scattered.

Edwin, who'd been firing the Gatling gun, was slumped over the edge of the wagon, half his head gone.

Hector Junior, who'd stayed at the wagon with him, lay in the dirt.

The horses harnessed to the wagon must have been trained to ignore gunfire, Spence reckoned. They just stood there, shuffling and snorting, and Spence reckoned they'd stay there till kingdom come unless somebody told them to move.

Spence had no idea which direction the bullets that had killed Edwin and Hector Junior and Dwight had come from. For all he knew, there were deputies all over, shooting at the bank.

He ran around the corner of the bank, into Freemont Street. The first thing he did was stumble over one of the people Edwin had shot with the Gatling gun. The fellow must have been hit seven or eight times, and had been near enough torn in half. There were a dozen or so bodies like that. Men and women. Spence felt sick, but he couldn't stop. If anybody realized he'd been one of the gang, he'd be facing the noose again.

He put his head down and ran. Rounding the next corner, he expected to find a load of people cowering there, but the street was empty except for a lone horse, all saddled up and standing in the shade, twitching its ears and waiting to get told what to do next.

It was the horse Abel Cole had ridden into town on, a chestnut mare with a white blaze on its face.

The mare shied a little as Spence came up to it, but he pulled down his bandanna and cooed at it and said, 'Steady, girl,' and it stayed still enough for him to grab the reins and haul himself up onto its back.

He rode out of town. Not too fast. Not like he had anything to do with the bank robbery and the slaughter at all.

Nobody stopped him, nobody challenged him. No more than a couple of people even looked in his direction.

Spence rode back to the Coles' hideout in the canyon. His belongings were there. It wasn't much, but it was everything he had.

When he arrived he had the bank manager's Smith & Wesson ready to hand, in case he had to draw it. He didn't know what reception he'd get from the women when he arrived back alone.

Edith, the woman who'd found him down at the pool with Mercy, saw him first. She appeared out of the door of the house, a shotgun in her hands, but she didn't point it at him. She kept it aimed down at the ground and said, 'Where's the rest of them? They dead?'

'I reckon,' he said. He told her what had happened, as much as he knew.

'You should've killed Ma,' she said. 'She'll come after you, for sure.'

'They'll hang her.'

'I wouldn't bet money on that. If there's a way of getting away, she'll do it. She ain't the kind that's easy to kill.'

Edith didn't seem too fussed about her man being killed. The other two women, Beth and Annie, had appeared too. They weren't fussed either.

'You ain't angry about your men being dead?' said Spence.

Beth said, 'We don't need them. We always managed better when they weren't around.'

'What will you do now?' asked Spence.

'I'm staying here,' said Edith. 'People mostly ain't got no use for me, and I ain't got no use for them. I like it out here. We can kill for food, and there are plants we can eat, growing right here in the canyon. We got enough ammunition to last years. Anyway, Beth knows how to trap. We won't starve.'

'What'll you do if Ma turns up?'

The women looked at each other. Beth said, 'She'll know you've been here, and she won't like it much when she finds out we didn't even try and kill you. She'll try to whip us, or kill us. We'll kill her, if we can. But make no mistake, till you know she's dead, you better sleep with one eye open.'

'I'll do just that,' he said. 'Mind if I keep the horse?'

'It's yours,' said Edith. 'We got a couple of mules. If we need to ride anywhere, they'll do just fine.'

So Spence collected his belongings and headed south, to the border.

He thought that once he'd got into Mexico his troubles would be over, but as it turned out he thought wrong.

He got across the border without any trouble. There weren't any patrols or fences like he thought there might be. Not even a sign. He rode along a desert track, and when he got to the next town he asked the first person he met how far it was to the border, and they told him he was in Mexico already.

He decided he'd spend the night in a rooming house. It was a long time since he'd spent the night in anything like a real bed. He was used to sharing a bunkhouse with a dozen or so other cowmen, but that was luxury compared to what he'd had to endure

76

recently: sleeping on the dirt, under the stars, or trying to sleep in that cell in Gila Creek, or on the floor in the Cole place, listening to Ma snore.

Spence kicked off his boots and lay on the bed. The sun was low, the sky outside the window a deep blue.

He could hear the sounds of the Mexican town, whatever its name was. Kids playing, a dog yapping, a burro padding by on the hard-packed earth, a couple of *señors* talking in Spanish.

He closed his eyes and went to sleep.

When he woke up the room was in darkness. The muzzle of a gun was being pressed to his head, and a man was saying, 'Wake up, Zeke. Looks like I finally caught up with you. I've been hunting you all the way from Flagstaff.'

Spence said, 'I don't know who you are, Mister. But you got the wrong man. And I don't mind telling you, I'm getting sick and tired of people mistaking me for this Zeke Tolan.'

The man said, 'The hammer on this here gun is cocked and ready to fire. One little squeeze on the trigger, when you wake up next, you'll be waking up in Hades. So don't take me for a fool.'

Spence wasn't rightly sure where Hades was, but it didn't sound good.

The man with the gun backed off. 'Light that there candle by the side of the bed, and do it slow.'

There was a small table next to the bed, and a stub of a candle and matches on the top of it. Spence lit the candle.

The man studied Spence, and Spence studied him back. The man was about average height, fair-haired and blue-eyed, and dressed like a tenderfoot. He didn't talk like a tenderfoot, though. He sounded tough. He sounded like a fellow who knew how to use that .45 he was holding.

The man peered at Spence, and a look of doubt passed over his face. 'Turn your head,' he said.

Spence turned his head towards the candle.

'Not that way,' said the man. 'The other way.'

So Spence turned his head the other way.

The man gave a low whistle. Then he said, 'Well, I'll be damned! You *ain't* Zeke Tolan!'

'That's what I been telling everybody,' said Spence. 'Now, would you mind lowering that hog-leg?'

The man looked at the gun, like he'd forgotten he was holding it. He holstered the .45 and grinned. 'Why, I apologise for waking you so rudely, fella,' he said. 'You see, I had good information it was Zeke Tolan who was sleeping in this room. At least, I *thought* it was good information. But I can see how the mistake was made. You sure look like him. You could almost be his twin. Mind telling me your name?'

'I don't mind,' said Spence. 'But where I come from, it's considered polite to introduce yourself before you ask another fellow's name. Who are you, fella?'

The man didn't stop grinning. He reached into his jacket with the hand that wasn't holding the .45 any more and pulled out a small rectangle of white card.

He flicked it over to Spence. 'The name's Harris. George Harris. I'm a Pinkerton man.'

Spence picked up the card, and sure enough it said the man was George Harris of the Pinkerton Detective Agency.

'Tolan has been a thorn in the side of the railroads and the banks these last few years, and I've been sent to track him down. Looks like I was given a false trail.'

'I'm Danny Spence,' said Spence. 'I've been working ranches since I was a kid, and I was on my way to California to see the ocean when I made the mistake of passing through a place called Gila Creek. You heard of it?'

Harris stopped grinning. 'I've heard of Gila Creek. Every lawman in the country has heard of Gila Creek. There was a massacre. Almost the whole town slaughtered with a Gatling gun.'

Spence nodded. 'That's right. I was there. I was about to get hung alongside of a man named Abel Cole, when his ma and his brothers came to rescue him. It was them who had that Gatling gun. They took me along with them, on account of they thought I might come in useful. This Zeke Tolan's supposed to be a master safe cracker.'

'That he is,' said Harris. Then his hand twitched, like he was thinking of drawing his .45 again. 'Were you there in Paradise Flats? That was a Gatling gun too. And a load of dynamite. They caught or killed the Cole gang, I heard.'

Spence told him what had happened in Paradise

Flats, how he'd been forced to go along, and Harris's hand stopped twitching.

Then Spence said, 'Have you met this Zeke Tolan? Everybody else swears I'm exactly like him, but you can tell just by looking at me that I ain't him.'

'Quick, ain't ya?' said Harris. 'Yeah, I know him pretty well. We grew up together in the same town. When we were eight years old we had a fight and I bit his right earlobe off.'

Spence wasn't expecting that. 'Ain't it generally known that he has his right earlobe bit off?'

'It says so on the wanted posters. Some of them. But people don't always read them as close as they should. But I'd guess it don't show that much now. The teeth marks will have smoothed over some. It's had a long time to heal. I'd guess people wouldn't even notice the lobe was missing unless they compared his right ear with his left. Some people don't have any earlobes at all.'

'Pinkerton's gave you the job of catching him, on account of you grew up with him?'

'That's right. With me it's personal. His ma was a good woman. Like a real mother to me, after my ma died. But when he started robbing and killing, it broke her heart. He killed her too, sure as if he'd put a bullet in her.'

Spence studied the card with Harris's name on it, flicked the corner with his thumbnail. 'You going to go back up to Arizona now, tell everybody that Danny Spence ain't Zeke Tolan?' he asked. 'You could tell them that if they see a man who looks like Zeke Tolan, but has two earlobes, then it's me, and I'd sure appreciate it if they didn't hang me.'

'I'll tell them.'

'Much obliged.'

But Harris didn't leave. He scratched his chin, deep in thought. Eventually he said, 'You ever heard of a man named Hernando Ortiz?'

'Nope,' said Spence. 'Who's he?'

'Another fellow I'm hoping to catch up with. Also, Ortiz is a friend of Tolan's.'

'Yeah?'

'There's a reward out for him. Five thousand dollars, for information leading to his capture, dead or alive.'

'That's more money than I'm liable to see in my whole lifetime,' said Spence. 'Good luck. Hope you get it.'

'I can't claim it,' said Harris. 'Not with me being a Pinkerton man. But you could. You could claim that five thousand dollars. It would set you up for life.'

'That it would,' agreed Spence.

Harris dug around in his jacket, found a cheroot, stuck it in his mouth. 'You want one?'

'No thanks,' said Spence.

Harris lit the cheroot and blew a cloud of yellow-brown smoke at the ceiling. 'I've got a proposition to make to you.'

'I reckoned you were working around to something,' said Spence.

Harris sucked in more smoke, blew it out in a perfect 'O' that hung in the air above them. 'How do you feel about being Zeke Tolan just a little while longer?'

CHAPTER TEN

The next day, a hundred miles south-west, Zeke Tolan and his gang rode into a little town called San Miguel, which till a couple of months earlier had boasted a population of about five hundred. But then the soldiers had come and killed most of the menfolk, in retaliation for attacks by Pancho Villa's Division of the North. The menfolk hadn't had anything to do with the attacks, but that didn't matter. They'd been killed anyway. The soldiers had shot them in the town square, and left the bodies there for the womenfolk to bury.

About the only man left in the town was the priest, Don Perez, who was seventy-three years old, but looked about a hundred.

When Tolan's gang arrived on their horses, all the women scurried into their houses and bolted the doors and windows. But Tolan and his gang weren't interested in the women. Not yet, anyway. They headed straight for the church, and when they got there, Tolan got off his horse and went inside.

The church was big as a cathedral. It had a high, vaulted ceiling and a dome. Tolan stood in the middle of the deserted church and looked up at the ceiling, and up at the windows with their panes of coloured glass, and up at the painted wooden figure nailed to the cross behind the altar, and at the painted figure of the Virgin Mary to one side of the altar, and the figure of Saint Michael the archangel, who the town was named after, on the other side. And he looked at the carved wooden candlesticks in front of the altar and shook his head sadly.

Tolan found the old priest in one of the small back rooms, reading his Bible.

'*Buenos días, padre,*' said Tolan.

The old man looked at him, and said in English, 'You bring your gun into the house of the Lord? You should be ashamed. But a man like you does not know shame.'

Tolan grinned. 'Now, how can you say such a terrible thing? You ain't never laid eyes on me before.'

The priest said, 'I have seen men like you before many times. You are evil. I see it in your eyes.'

Tolan laughed. 'Well, I ain't going to contradict you, Padre. That would be rude. Now, the reason I'm here is, the last time I paid a visit to this magnificent church of yours, there was a couple of gold candlesticks out there. Now all I see are a pair of wooden ones. What I want to know is, where are the gold candlesticks? And don't tell me the *federales* or the revolutionaries took 'em, because I know that'll be a lie. You Mexicans are mighty religious, and nobody is going to risk bringing the wrath of the Almighty down on them by stealing from a church. But like you already said, I'm evil, so I don't care about things like that.'

The old man shook his head. 'I shall never tell you.'

'I kind of reckoned you'd say that,' said Tolan.

About the same time Tolan was spelling things out to the old priest, the Pinkerton man, Harris, was paying another visit to Spence's room. This time he brought with him another man, a fellow named Hubert Jeffries.

Jeffries was big and solid-looking with slicked-back grey hair and ice-blue eyes.

'Mr Jeffries is a Texas Ranger,' said Harris.

'It's an honour to meet you, Mr Jeffries,' said Spence. 'Afraid there ain't much room for you gentlemen to sit, what with there being only the bed and the one chair.'

'Don't you worry about that, Mr Spence,' said Jeffries. 'I'm happy to remain standing. Mr Harris tells me that you also hail from the Lone Star state.'

'I sure do,' said Spence, shaking his hand. 'My ma told me I was born somewhere in the High Plains, and I ain't never had any reason to doubt her.'

'The pleasure's all mine,' said Jeffries. 'And now we've all got acquainted, why don't we get down to business? I know this may sound a mite crazy, but Mr

Harris and I want you to pretend to be Zeke Tolan, and get inside the hacienda of a man named Hernando Ortiz.'

Harris had already told Spence how Ortiz was a murdering *bandito* who, up till about five years ago, had killed and robbed his way across five states north of the border. But no US lawman could touch him. He had friends in the Mexican government. He also had influential American friends – businessmen who paid him well to keep things running smoothly in Ortiz's part of Sonora, where these businessmen had a lot of money tied up in agriculture and whatever. And these businessmen didn't care how many Americans he'd killed, or how many American banks he'd robbed some time back. Ortiz spent most of his time in his hacienda, which was like a fortress, guarded by a dozen or so *federales*.

'Hernando Ortiz and Zeke Tolan met a few years back,' said Harris. 'They rode with the same gang for a while. If anybody has a chance of getting into that fortified hacienda of his, it's you.'

'And what do you want me to do once I've got inside this hacienda?' asked Spence. 'I killed Abel Cole, but I didn't like it much. I don't want to kill anybody else, if it's all the same to you. Not even for five thousand dollars.'

'We don't expect you to,' said Jeffries. 'All we want you to do is put a little something in their water. The hacienda has a well, and that's where they get all their water from.'

'And what exactly do you want me to put in their water?' asked Spence.

'Opium,' said Jeffries. 'You've heard of opium?'

'Sure I've heard of opium,' said Spence. 'They put it in laudanum, the stuff folk have for toothache and suchlike. It makes you kind of drunk.'

'That's right,' said Jeffries. 'I'm going to give you a crate of good whiskey, which you'll give to Ortiz as a gift. But I'll also give you a couple of bottles of rotgut whiskey. You'll tell anybody who asks that this whiskey is for yourself. One of these bottles won't contain whiskey, it'll contain powdered opium. And when you get the chance, you'll pour the opium into the well. It won't be long before all the soldiers will be sleeping like babes. Then you open the gates. We come in, grab Ortiz and take him back to the United States, where he'll finally get a taste of American justice.'

Spence mulled over the proposition. Five thousand dollars was a lot of money. But it wouldn't do him any good if he was dead. 'If this Ortiz fellow is such a good friend of Tolan's that he'll let him into his hacienda, won't he see I ain't Tolan? Soon as he sees I don't have an earlobe bitten off, he'll know I'm not the real thing.'

Harris said, 'Tolan grows his hair long. Carlos probably hasn't even had a good look at his ears.'

Jeffries said, 'You'll be doing your patriotic duty. There'll be a lot of folk in the United States who'll be very pleased we got their hands on Señor Ortiz.'

The thought of all that money was sure tempting.

With five thousand dollars in his pocket he could buy himself passage on a ship and see the world, have himself some adventures like in all those stories he'd read.

'With luck,' said Harris, 'You'll only have to be inside that compound a day or so. What do you say?'

Spence shrugged. 'All right,' he said. 'I'll do it.'

'Good man,' said Jeffries. He shook Spence's hand again. 'I've no doubt you'll do the great state of Texas proud.'

'I'll sure do my best,' replied Spence.

CHAPTER ELEVEN

Zeke Tolan's gang had grabbed as many of the town's women and children as they could lay their hands on, and got them inside the church.

Tolan had dragged the priest to the pulpit and made him stand there while the gang made the women and children sit on the hard wooden pews.

Tolan said to the priest, 'I reckon you are in intelligent man, and you'll have probably figured out by now what's going to happen if you don't tell me where those gold candlesticks are. But in case you're dumber than I think you are, I'll spell it out for you. I'm going to ask you where the candlesticks are, and you'll have three seconds to answer. If you don't answer, I'll shoot a member of this here congregation. And if you tell me a lie, I'll shoot one of 'em. You understand?'

The old priest nodded.

'Don't tell him, Padre!' shouted a woman on the second row. 'He is bluffing! He would not be so low as to kill somebody in the house of the. . . .'

Zeke Tolan already had his six-gun in his hand. He aimed, fired, and hit the woman in the chest. She slumped forward, dead.

'Anybody else reckon I'm bluffing?' he asked.

The children started wailing. The women tried their best to hush them.

'No?' said Tolan. 'Good.' He turned back to the priest. 'Tell me where them gold candlesticks are,' he said.

The priest told him.

It took Spence and Harris and Jeffries three days to ride to Hernando Ortiz's hacienda. Harris and Jeffries escorted him to within a mile of the place, to make sure Spence didn't lose his nerve. With them were a half-dozen Americanos, all dressed as Mexicans, who Jeffries said were all Rangers.

'Remember, you'll be doing the United States a great service, helping to bring Ortiz to justice,' said Jeffries.

'Yeah, so you said,' Spence replied.

They were on a high bluff overlooking the hacienda. From here, Spence could see down into a wide, flat plain, and in the middle of it was Ortiz's fortified compound: a twelve-foot high wall enclosing about ten acres of ground, a long low building in the middle of it.

It was an hour or so before sunset, the sky turning pink in the west.

'We'll be up here, watching the main gates,' said

Harris. 'I'd guess that if you put the opium in that sometime during the night, by late morning every person in that place will have drunk some of the water from out of the doctored well. They'll have consumed enough opium not to know what's happening, or care. Just remember to only drink the water you've brought with you, in your canteen. When you open the gates, we'll ride in and grab Ortiz. With luck nobody will have to fire a single shot.'

They all shook hands again, and Spence rode down into the valley. He had a mule with him, and on the mule's back was the crate of good whiskey he was to present to his 'old friend' Ortiz as a gift. In his saddle-bags were the two bottles of rotgut, one of which contained the powdered opium.

When he finally made it to the main gates, a *federale* opened a hatch, peered out at Spence and said, '*¿Quién eres tú? ¿Qué deseas?*'

He was being asked who he was and what he wanted. '*Mi nombre es Zeke Tolan. Soy amigo del señor Ortiz,*' he replied.

The *federale* closed the hatch. Spence sat out in the hot Mexican sun on his horse, and was just starting to wonder if he really knew what he was getting himself into when the hatch opened again and a different face peered out.

This face was older and had a white goatee beard. When it saw Spence it broke into a big, gold-toothed grin, and shouted at somebody to open the gates.

The gates swung open and the owner of the face

shouted in English, 'Well, I'll be a son of a bitch! If it ain't my old friend Zeke! Come on in here, and let me get a good look at you!' He spoke English with barely a trace of a Mexican accent.

Spence rode his horse through the gates, and the mule trotted along behind.

The gates were closed again, and Spence got off his horse.

The fellow with the goatee, who Spence reckoned had to be Ortiz himself, grabbed him in a bear hug. Then he held Spence at arms' length and squinted at his face, frowning.

'You look different,' said the man.

'Yeah? How's that?' asked Spence.

The man squinted at him a little more and grinned again, saying, 'You got a haircut! I ain't never seen you with short hair before. And you got thinner.'

'I been doing a lot of riding,' said Spence. He nodded over to the mule. 'I brought you present. A whole crate of whiskey.'

The man slapped Spence's shoulder. 'You're a true *amigo*! So, what brings you to Sonora?'

Spence shrugged. 'Passing through. Besides, things were starting to get a mite dangerous for me north of the border. I got lawmen and Pinkerton men and just about everybody else on my trail. So I thought I'd head south, see if I couldn't lose 'em. And since I was in the vicinity, I thought I'd pay a visit on my old pal Hernando. Hope you don't mind?'

'Of course I don't mind,' said Hernando. 'Come on

inside the house. We can sip whiskey and talk over old times.'

'Yeah,' said Spence. 'Let's do that.'

'You recall that time in Laramie, Ed Kane got punched by that saloon girl so hard, she knocked him on his ass?' said Ortiz. 'Funniest thing I ever saw.'

'Yeah,' said Spence. 'I seem to recall, I laughed fit to bust.'

They were sitting in big fat overstuffed leather armchairs in Ortiz's house. Ortiz was a rich fellow, all right. Spread out on the floors were brightly coloured, intricately patterned oriental rugs that dazzled the eye. There were paintings on the walls of folk wearing a lot of silk and jewels, even the men, and the paintings all had fancy gold frames. And Ortiz seemed to have a taste for statues of naked women. Everywhere Spence looked there was another naked woman, in gold or marble or whatever, but mostly gold.

There was a lot of gold around. Ortiz wore a gold ring on each finger, and had a gold medallion on a gold chain around his neck. He even had gold teeth.

They drank the good whiskey that Spence had brought with him. Ortiz was delighted with the gift. As for Spence, he'd never tasted whiskey so good. It slipped down like honey. They drank it out of crystal glasses. Spence had never even seen a crystal glass before, let alone drunk out of one.

'You said you were going to marry her, then and there,' said Ortiz. 'Just because she'd knocked Ed

Kane on his ass. You demanded we find a preacher. I never seen anybody as drunk as you were.'

'Yeah, that was quite a night,' said Spence.

It seemed like Ortiz knew Tolan better than Harris and Jeffries thought he did. But Ortiz still seemed to think Spence was Tolan, so maybe it was going to be all right after all. Spence had begun to worry, while they were talking and drinking, that maybe his voice wasn't like Tolan's, or he didn't move the same way Tolan did, but Ortiz didn't say anything about that. So Spence reckoned he must talk and move something like Tolan, not just look like him. Close enough, anyway. Then again, according to Harris it had been a few years since the last time Ortiz and Tolan had met, and memories get hazy, and people change anyway.

For whatever reason, Ortiz didn't give any sign that he thought he was anybody except Zeke Tolan.

Eventually the tall mahogany grandfather clock in the corner of the room sounded midnight. They'd been talking for hours. Ortiz said, 'I must be getting old. I can't drink all night like I used to. I need to get to bed. I'll have my man show you to your room. Your saddle-bags are already in there.'

Ortiz picked up a tiny silver bell that sat on a table next to his armchair. He shook it, and it gave out a tinkling noise.

Barely had the sound of the bell faded than a huge man appeared in the doorway. He must have been close to seven feet tall, and broad with it, and each of his arms was as thick as one of Spence's legs. He was completely bald, and had a deep scar that ran diagonally across his face, all the way from just below his right eye, across his upper lip, to the angle of his jaw on the opposite side.

Ortiz turned to Spence. 'This is Bracho. His father cut him in a drunken rage when he was twelve years old. I do not know why. I don't know if Bracho knows either. In revenge, Bracho killed him with his bare hands while the man slept.'

'He killed his own father?' asked Spence.

Ortiz nodded, grinning. 'At that moment Bracho discovered he enjoyed strangling people. As you can see, his hands are twice the size of any normal man's. I once saw him pick up a fellow with just one of those hands, pin him against a wall and crush his windpipe. He is magnificent, is he not?'

'He sure is,' said Spence. 'You just make sure he knows that if there's a fight, I'm on his side.'

Ortiz laughed. 'Don't worry. I would never let any harm come to my good old friend Zeke Tolan.'

CHAPTER TWELVE

Bracho showed Spence to his room. The room itself was plain enough, with whitewashed walls and a polished wood floor, but the bed and the rest of the furniture was all expensive-looking, all exquisitely carved out of dark wood.

After the giant had left him alone, Spence went over to the window and looked out.

The house was only one-storey high, and the room was at the back of the house, so all Spence needed to do, if he had a mind to, was climb over the windowsill and he'd be in a small grove of olive trees that grew out there.

He turned down the oil lamp Bracho had lit for him and waited at the window, looking out, listening for noises.

He couldn't hear anything out there apart from the clicking of the cicadas, and – way, way off – the howl of a coyote.

Spence was listening for the sound of a guard patrolling the interior of the compound, but if there was anybody out there, they must have been wearing moccasins.

He waited a while longer, till he heard Ortiz's grandfather clock chime half past the hour.

He grabbed the bottle containing the powdered opium out of his saddle-bag and climbed out of the window.

Spence stood in the olive grove, waiting some more, peering out through the branches at the open ground in the centre of the compound.

The moon was big and low.

He could make out the well, right in the middle, with its low wall and the winch for the bucket.

Over to his right was a second house, which Spence reckoned was the barracks for the *federales* who'd been given the job of guarding Ortiz, and over to his left were the stables. There was a fourth building, not far from the barracks, and Spence figured that to be the armoury.

Spence assumed there was a guard watching the gates, like there'd been earlier. There might also be other guards, posted on all sides of the compound. But they'd been looking out, watching for anybody who might be trying to sneak up to the compound from outside – the guards wouldn't be looking *into* the compound.

All in all, despite the moonlight, he reckoned he had a pretty good chance of getting to the well and back unobserved.

Or so he reckoned.

There was only one way of finding out for sure.

CHAPTER THIRTEEN

A few hours earlier, when Ma Cole finally woke up, she was lying on a narrow bed with her right hand cuffed to the bed's metal frame.

All she could see was a white-painted ceiling and white-painted walls.

It looked like she was in some kind of a cell, except that it had an ordinary-looking wooden door, not a metal door.

The last thing she remembered, she was in the bank manager's office, and Zeke Tolan had just shot her in the leg. She must have passed out, either through blood loss or the pain of getting shot, or both.

She'd been awake for an hour before a man came into the room and looked down at her. They stared at each other. He was fat and sixty, with a gleaming pink scalp and wire-framed spectacles.

'So, you're awake,' he said. 'I'm the doctor. You're in Paradise Flats hospital. And the only reason you've been kept alive is so we can hang you. I dug the bullet out of your leg, and bandaged it up. I wished I'd had an excuse to amputate your leg, but to my eternal disappointment the damage wasn't that bad. You in pain?'

Ma Cole didn't reply. Just kept staring at him. She was in a great deal of pain, but she wasn't going to tell him that.

'I hope you're in pain,' he said. 'I hope you're in so much pain you can hardly bear it. But I'm a doctor, and I've sworn an oath to take good care of my patients – not that swearing oaths and suchlike will mean anything to somebody like you, you murdering bitch. I reckon you'll be in a great deal of pain, and despite the fact I'd rather let you lie there in agony, as a doctor I'll have to waste good morphine on you.'

He left the room and came back a few minutes later with a hypodermic syringe. 'There's a deputy outside,' he said, nodding to the door, which he'd left half-open. 'He lost a lot of his friends when you and your damned sons blew up the sheriff's office, and he'd dearly like an excuse to finish you himself. You understand me, bitch?'

Still she didn't answer, just stared.

The doctor leaned over her and prepared to inject her with the morphine.

Deputy Wynn sat outside Ma Cole's room. He and the other remaining deputies had been taking turns guarding the room, making sure she didn't escape, and making sure none of the good citizens of Paradise

Flats killed her before the hangman did. He'd been sitting in the corridor a few hours now, and the bitch had been asleep most of that time.

She'd been pumped full of morphine when the bullet had been dug out of her leg, and she'd been unconscious till not long ago. The fellow who'd dug the bullet out of her leg, Dr Mead, had gone in there and found she was awake.

Mead had come out again and said, 'She's woken up. I'm going to get some more morphine.'

Wynn had said, 'OK, Doc.' He didn't get up and look at her. He wasn't that curious to see what she looked like awake. He'd already seen enough of her ugly face when she was asleep. So he sat back in his chair and carried on reading his newspaper. He wasn't worried about Ma Cole sneaking up behind him or anything like that, evil as she was. For one thing, she was handcuffed securely to the bed, and he had the key in his vest pocket. For another thing, she was probably still half full of morphine from the last time she'd been given it. And for yet another thing, there wasn't any way she was any kind of a threat, not with a big hole in her leg like that. And lastly, she was a woman. A sizeable woman, sure. But still a woman.

And Deputy Conner had never met a woman he couldn't handle.

The doctor came back with the hypodermic syringe full of morphine and went into the room, and then he said something to the woman that the deputy didn't quite hear, and then there was silence for a few seconds, presumably while he pumped the drug into her.

'Deputy, can you come in here and hold this bitch down?'

The doctor sounded exasperated. Probably hadn't expected her to struggle, Wynn thought.

He folded his newspaper and laid it on the floor under the chair and went into the room to hold the woman down.

When he went into the room he saw the doctor leaning over her, almost lying on top of her – trying to hold the bitch down, Wynn guessed.

He went up to the bed and said, 'OK, Doc – I'll take over from here.'

But the doctor didn't move. Instead a hand snaked out from underneath the doctor's body and stabbed Wynn in the thigh with the syringe.

Before Wynn could draw his gun or yell, half the syringe full of morphine had been pumped into him. He pulled away and looked down and saw the syringe still hanging out of his leg. Then his vision went kind of hazy, the floor swung up to hit him in the side of the face, then nothing.

CHAPTER FOURTEEN

Ma Cole pushed the doctor's body off her and he rolled onto the floor, on top of the unconscious deputy.

As soon as the doctor had leaned over her to administer the morphine, she'd grabbed him with the hand that wasn't shackled to the bed and slammed his head into the wall. His eyes went blank. She didn't know if he was dead or just knocked cold, and she didn't care.

She kept the doctor's body lying on top of her, so it would look from the door like he was trying to pin her down, and growled, in a deep approximation of his voice, 'Deputy, can you come in here and hold this bitch down?'

When the deputy got close enough to the bed she stabbed him in the leg with the syringe and pressed the plunger. . . .

Ma Cole rolled off the bed, and – again using her

unshackled left hand – reached for the syringe, still sticking out of the deputy's leg. She injected some of the morphine into her own leg, enough to take the edge off the pain, then she went through the deputy's pockets till she found the key for the handcuffs.

She unlocked the handcuffs and started peeling off the deputy's clothes.

While she'd been unconscious, Ma had been undressed and put in some kind of cotton shroud. She couldn't walk around looking like that. The doctor was fat, but he wasn't tall, she would never be able to fit into his clothes. But the deputy was a big fellow, she could fit into his.

Feeling light-headed on account of the morphine, Ma put on the deputy's clothes, but his boots didn't fit her. The doctor's feet were about the right size though, so she squeezed her feet into his patent leather shoes.

She strapped the deputy's gunbelt around her waist. He had a Colt .45 in the holster, which suited her fine.

She tucked her hair up into the deputy's Stetson and pulled the hat down at the front so she could peer out from under the brim.

As she left the room, a nurse came around the corner of the hallway and saw her. The nurse looked at her, and it took her a moment to realize that the person in man's clothes was the woman who was supposed to be shackled to the bed. She opened her mouth to scream, but Ma pistol-whipped her before she could make a sound, and she crumpled to the floor.

Ma discovered she was on the second floor of the hospital building. She made her way down a staircase at the rear, and left through a back door.

The back door led out onto an alleyway. There wasn't anybody around.

She kept to the backstreets of Paradise Flats, wandering around till she found a livery stable. When she entered the stable she found a man feeding the horses. He was an old fellow, thin as a reed, with watery eyes.

'Any of these horses for sale?'

'No,' he said, looking at her, not sure if he was talking to a man or a woman.

'Any of them for hire, then?' Ma Cole looked around. She couldn't see any other people, just the horses.

'Well, I . . .'

The old man didn't get any further. She pistol-whipped him like she'd done the nurse, tied him up with some rope she found, stuffed a kerchief into his mouth and saddled up one of the horses.

She found the office, stole the cash from the tin box on the desk, and rode out of town.

When she got back to the vicinity of the hideout, she dismounted at the edge of the canyon and looked down into it, watching for movement.

From here she couldn't quite see the house, but she

could see smoke rising up in a straight line through the warm, still air.

Somebody was cooking.

She tethered the horse and crept down into the canyon, working her way around so that she would approach the house from the back.

She was within twenty feet of the back of the house when a voice behind her snapped, 'Get your hands up!'

It was Beth's voice.

Ma didn't put her hands up in the air. Instead she said, 'Guess you don't recognize me in my borrowed duds. It's me, Ma.'

She turned round.

'I said, *get your hands up!*'

But still Ma didn't put your hands up. She twisted her mouth into something like a smile and said, 'You going deaf, girl? I said it's me, Ma.'

'I can see who you are, well enough,' said Beth, her voice shaking with fear. She was pointing a shotgun at Ma's belly, and the shotgun was shaking too.

'What's wrong with you, girl?' barked Ma. 'If you don't put that gun down this instant, I'll tan your hide for you!'

Beth shook her head. 'I ain't doing nothing you say any more,' she said. 'And if you don't put your hands up, I'll fill you full of buckshot!'

Ma laughed. 'Well, well! When did you suddenly get yourself some guts, little girl? You chose the wrong person to get brave with. Now, I'll tell you one last time, put down that goddamn shotgun!'

Beth was so scared she thought she might faint. She shouted, 'Edith! She's here! Ma came back! She's here!'

Edith came out of the house, and she had a shotgun too. Annie came out also, trailing behind her, but she didn't appear to be carrying any gun.

Ma Cole said to Edith, 'Where are my boys?'

Edith aimed the shotgun at her head, so now Ma had two shotguns pointed at her. Edith said, 'They're all dead, we reckon. We heard what happened at Paradise Flats. Abel and Dwight and Edwin and Hector Junior are all dead, I know that for sure. I don't know about Virgil, but I reckon he's dead too. I hope so. We ain't seen nothing of him. We ain't seen anything of Bradley or O'Brien either.'

A pain a thousand times greater than the pain in her leg coursed through Ma's soul. She felt like a fist had grabbed her heart and was crushing it. 'To hell with Bradley or O'Brien,' shrieked Ma. 'They ain't my flesh and blood!' Then she said, 'How come you know so much?'

Edith didn't answer.

Ma said, 'It was that sonofabitch Zeke Tolan. That snake was the one shot me in the leg. He was here, wasn't he?'

Ma went for the Colt .45 at her hip, at the same time throwing herself onto the ground. Behind her, Beth's shotgun boomed. The pellets flew over Ma's head and peppered a cactus sixty feet away. Ma fired at Edith first, reckoning that out of the two women aiming guns at her, Edith was the better shot. The .45's bullet hit Edith in the chest and knocked her clean off her feet.

Even before Edith crashed onto the dirt, Ma had twisted around and fired another shot before Beth could. Her second bullet grazed Beth's shoulder and spun her round.

'Goddamn whore!' yelled Ma, scrambling to her feet. The morphine was wearing off again. She limped over to where Beth lay bleeding and pointed the Colt at her head.

Before she could squeeze the trigger, there was a boom, and a bullet hissed past Ma's ear.

'Leave her alone, you damn bitch!' yelled Annie. She'd pulled a revolver from out of her coat pocket, an old Army Colt that used to be Ma's late husband's. She was only a tiny thing, not even five feet tall, and the gun was near as big as she was.

Ma was about to aim her gun at Annie, take her chances, but then Beth, lying on the ground, stamped her foot against the back of Ma's good knee.

Ma landed heavily on the ground.

'You've had this coming, you bitch!' yelled Annie. Annie had been bullied by Ma more than anybody else had, and hated her so much she wasn't thinking straight. She fired the Army Colt again, and didn't even think about whether she might hit Beth if the shot went wide. Which it did.

The bullet missed Ma and went straight through

Beth's heart.

'Beth!' yelled Annie.

Ma snarled, 'None of you useless *putas* ever could shoot worth a damn.'

Ma shot Annie straight between the eyes.

She scrambled back up the side of the canyon and brought the stolen horse down into the shade and gave it oats and water. She was going to need it later. Then she went into the adobe and found a bottle of whiskey. She lay on top of the coffin that contained the mummified remains of her late husband Hector and started to get drunk.

'I'm gonna get Zeke Tolan,' she said. 'I'm going to cut off his head and hang it up on the wall above the bed here, so it'll be the last thing I see every night. You hear me, Hector? I'll get that sonofabitch if it's the last thing I ever do.'

CHAPTER FIFTEEN

Spence was about to step out from beneath the branches of the olive trees, onto the open ground, when he heard the muffled cry of a woman coming from somewhere over to his right.

Then there were the sounds of a struggle, and a man grunted, '*¡Quédate quieto, puta! ¡Sabes que lo quieres!*'

Lie still, you bitch! You know you want it!

Spence dropped the bottle with the powdered opium in it and ran through the branches, tearing them aside, towards the struggle.

It was dark under those olive branches, black as pitch with shifting patches of moonlight filtering through. Spence saw one of Ortiz's *federales* holding a woman, maybe twenty years old, onto the ground. He'd torn open the front of her shirt, exposing her breasts. He lay on top of her and had a hand around her neck, choking her, and with his other hand he was pulling up her skirt. She kept squirming and trying to scream, and her eyes were wide and scared, nearly popping out of her skull.

Spence grabbed the collar of the man's tunic and hauled him up, and when he got him upright he punched the man in the jaw, knocking him flat.

The man didn't stay down long. He rolled up onto his feet, blood pouring out of his mouth. Spence had broken loose a couple of his teeth. The man spat out the teeth and screamed at Spence, something in Spanish that Spence didn't catch. Then from somewhere he pulled out a knife, a thin-bladed stiletto that glinted savagely.

The *federale* lunged at Spence.

Usually Spence drew the line at pistol-whipping people. He figured if you were in a fistfight, then you used your fists. Or your feet, if you had to. Maybe even your head. But if a fellow wanted to up the stakes by pulling a knife, from that point onwards, so far as Spence was concerned you could dispense with the niceties.

He pulled out his gun and as the federale dived at him with the stiletto, Spence dodged the blade and whacked the side of the fellow's head with the barrel. The *federale* went down and lay sprawled in the dirt.

But now there were a whole bunch of *federales* pouring out of the barracks and heading this way.

When they got to the olive trees, they saw their comrade lying on the ground, knocked cold, and Spence standing there with the gun still in his fist, and the woman with her shirt torn open. One of the *federales*, a fellow who looked a little older and tougher than the rest, said to Spence in English, 'What has happened here?'

Spence nodded at the man on the ground. 'This sonofabitch was trying to rape this woman.'

The man said, 'So? She is a whore.'

Spence said, 'I don't know about that, but she didn't want to get raped, and I wasn't going to stand by and let him do it.'

The man stared at Spence a second or two, then said, 'You are the Americano – the friend of Señor Ortiz? I saw you arrive today.'

'Yeah,' said Spence. 'I'm a friend of Señor Ortiz.'

The man, who Spence reckoned must be a sergeant or something, though he wasn't wearing his tunic, looked down at the fellow lying on the dirt and said, 'You pistol-whipped him?'

'He was coming at me with a knife.'

They could both see the stiletto lying on the ground near the unconscious man's hand.

The sergeant, or whatever, shook his head. 'Pereda is a fool. I tell him, if he keeps getting into fights, he should use his fists. One day he'll kill one of the other men with that little knife of his, and then I'll have to shoot him. It will be a waste of the time and effort spent training him, and it will be a waste of a bullet.' He barked an order at a couple of the other *federales*, and they picked up Pereda and dragged him back to the barracks.

Then the older, tougher man grinned at Spence

and said, 'Apologies for disturbing your night's rest, *señor*. But really, you should not concern yourself with trivial things, like a soldier raping a whore. Men will be men, after all.'

'The way I was raised,' said Spence, 'you ask nicely first. Even if the woman *is* a whore.'

The man looked at Spence curiously for a moment like he was some specimen in a jar that he hadn't come across before, then he turned and headed back to the barracks, shaking his head. The other *federales* went back to the barracks too, and soon it was just Spence and the woman, alone among the olive trees.

'Thank you,' said the woman, getting up off the ground and tying together the front of her shirt.

'You speak English?'

'Yes,' she said. 'I lived in the Arizona Territory for a while.'

'I spent a little time in Arizona myself,' he said. He didn't tell her he'd spent most of that time in a cell.

He looked out across the open centre of the quad-rangle, with the well in the middle. Somebody had an oil lamp lit in the barracks, and he could hear *federales* in there talking in Spanish, and a couple of them stood outside the door smoking cheroots. A few minutes ago everything had been quiet, he could have poured the opium into the well without anybody seeing. No chance now.

'I suppose *you* want me?' said the woman.

That wasn't uppermost in his mind at the moment. 'Thanks for the offer, but no thanks,' he said, thinking

112

that maybe in an hour or so all the soldiers who'd been woken up by the commotion would be back in their bunks again, asleep.

'You *don't* want me?' she asked.

'It's not that,' said Spence. 'It's just. . . . Why don't you go back home?'

'I have no home,' she said. 'The *federales* burned it down. They burned my entire village, and killed the men, and took the women as their *putas.*'

Spence had heard something about what had been going on down here in Mexico, and everything he'd heard told him it wasn't a good thing to be poor and Mexican.

'I'm sorry to hear that,' he said.

'They keep us in a room behind the barracks,' she said. 'Ortiz picks the best for himself, but when he's finished with them he gives them to his ogre of a bodyguard, Bracho. And then we do not see them again. The rest of us are used by the soldiers. I have been here ten days. Tonight I tried to escape. The soldiers are lazy, and they drink tequila every night till they are so drunk they are falling over. Some nights I think there is nobody guarding the hacienda at all, they are all drunk, and I hoped that tonight it would be so, but I was wrong. That soldier, he caught me and tried to rape me, but you saved me. None of the other men around here would. I want to thank you, but I have no other way of thanking you except with my body.'

'I appreciate, ma'am,' said Spence, 'And when this is all over, if you still feel the same way I'll be happy to oblige, but right now . . .'

'When *what* is all over?' she asked.

Spence could have bitten his own tongue off. Obviously he wasn't too good at subterfuge. The way he'd lived, men just pretty much said whatever was on their minds. 'No matter,' he said.

The soldiers were still smoking their cheroots outside the barracks, but it couldn't be long before they'd finished.

'The sergeant said you are a friend of Ortiz's,' said the woman.

'Yeah,' said Spence. 'That's right. I'm an old friend of Ortiz's.'

'Why are you a friend of such a man?' asked the woman. 'You are not like him. A friend of a man like Ortiz, if he saw a woman being raped, he would ignore it, or join in the fun. He would not save the woman and beat the man.'

'Yeah? You know that for a fact?'

'Yes, I do,' she said. 'When I was a child I would sit and study people, and think about what I saw. I thought deeply about many things, and read many books.'

'You did, huh?'

'My mother, she would say that I thought too much, and it was a habit I should stop, because it would only bring me unhappiness. I think she was right, and sometimes I try to stop thinking so much, but I cannot. I suppose I was made that way . . . I have seen many evil people. You are not one of them.'

114

'What happened to your ma?'

'She died of the cancer, while we were in Arizona Territory. I was still young, and could not take care of myself. A wealthy man offered to take care of me, but I did not want that, so I returned to my village, where my aunt lived. But now my aunt is dead too. The soldiers killed her, because she tried to defy them. So now I have nobody.'

She'd stepped towards him, and she wasn't in darkness any more. A beam of moonlight filtering through the olive branches hit her face, and he could see her clearly for the first time. She was pretty, except for her nose, which was broken and bruised, and twisted to one side.

'What happened to your nose?' Spence asked. 'The soldier do that?'

'No. I did that myself, a week ago. I thought that if I broke my nose I would not be pretty any more, and the soldiers would leave me alone. So I broke my nose with a rock. But it did not work, they carried on using me anyway.'

Spence heard screams coming from behind the barracks, and men cheering and laughing, shouting in Spanish. The woman heard them too.

'They are raping the women again,' she said. Then: 'Can I stay with you for tonight? It does not matter if you have me or not. I will sleep on the floor. Just do not send me back there.'

Spence reckoned the men wouldn't be asleep again for at least a couple of hours now. Then, with luck, there'd still be time before dawn for him to pour the opium into the well.

He found the bottle he'd let fall into the dirt, and led her in through the window, into his room.

Spence let the woman sleep in the bed. He lay down on the bed, over the sheet, and she lay beneath it.

She offered herself to him again, but he reckoned it was because she wanted to repay him, and though he wanted her, he figured it wouldn't be right, so he said no.

He lay in the dark and waited till the sounds from the barracks had died away, and everything was quiet again, apart from the clicking of the cicadas in the olive trees, and the howling of coyotes way off in the mountains.

Next to him, the woman hadn't stirred or made a sound for about an hour. He rolled off the bed silently and picked up the bottle of opium, and as he was about to climb back out through the window she said, 'Where are you going?'

'Go back to sleep,' he said.

'I knew you were not really a friend of Ortiz's,' she said. 'You have come here to kill him, haven't you? It is something to do with that bottle.'

He was standing in moonlight filtering in through the window. He couldn't see her so well, but obviously she could see him well enough.

'You had the bottle before,' she said, 'when you heard the soldier trying to rape me. I saw you pick it up off the dirt. Tell me what you are going to do. I

116

want to help.'

Spence reckoned the cat was out of the bag now anyway, he may as well tell her. He went over and sat on the edge of the bed. 'You're right. I'm not a friend of Ortiz's. I've never even met him before. But it seems I look like a friend of his, somebody he knew in America, a man named Zeke Tolan.'

'Is that possible? That you could look so like this Zeke Tolan man, you can fool Ortiz into thinking you are him?'

'If you'd told me a month ago that one man could look so much like another man he could fool somebody into thinking he really was the other fellow, I wouldn't have believed it. But that's the way it is. I spent the whole evening sipping whiskey with Ortiz, and he still thinks I'm Tolan.'

'What is in the bottle?'

'Opium. You know what opium is?'

'Of course.' She sounded insulted. 'It comes from poppies. They give it to people to stop pain. But some people become addicted to it, and cannot stop taking it. It gives people strange dreams, or so I have heard.'

She knew more about opium than he did. He didn't know they got it from poppies. It seemed crazy to him that a drug as powerful as opium was supposed to be could come out of a little red flower like a poppy. But then he remembered that whiskey came from barley and rye, and he'd heard about people who'd made hooch out of potatoes and all kinds of fruit and stuff, so why shouldn't they make drugs out of flowers?

'I'm going to sneak over to the well and pour this opium into the water,' he said. 'And then, after everybody's drunk on the opium, I'm going to open the gates of this here compound, and some friends of mine are going to come in and drag Ortiz back north of the border so he can stand trial.'

She wrapped her arms around him and kissed him. 'I knew you were a good man,' she told him. 'My heart told me so. I must help you to bring this evil man to justice.'

Spence felt her body pressed against him, and smelt the aroma of her, and it was all he could do to tear himself away.

'The best way you can help me is to stay here and keep quiet,' he told her, standing up.

She grabbed his sleeve. 'Wait! Now I know you are not this Zeke Tolan, I must know your real name.'

'My name's Daniel Spence. But my friends call me Danny.'

'May I call you Danny?'

'I guess you ought to, seeing as how we've been sharing a bed.'

'I am called Rosario,' she said.

'Delighted to make your acquaintance, Rosario,' he said. 'Now if you'll excuse me, I . . .'

Then the door burst open and a half-dozen soldiers poured into the room, and Ortiz's giant of a bodyguard, Bracho.

Bracho grabbed him by the neck and slammed him against a wall. Spence dropped the bottle of opium and it rolled across the floor.

Ortiz came in.

'What do you want?' rasped Spence, croaking some on account of Bracho's hand squeezing his throat.

Ortiz leaned in so his mouth was an inch from Spence's ear. 'I want to know who you are,' said Ortiz. 'Because you sure as hell ain't Zeke Tolan.'

CHAPTER SIXTEEN

Bracho hauled him out of the room, down a corridor and into the larger room where, a few hours earlier, Spence and Ortiz had been getting drunk.

Bracho threw Spence onto the floor in the middle of the room.

'I knew there was something off about you,' said Ortiz. 'You look like Tolan all right, and you talk pretty much like him, but there's something about the way you move that ain't right.'

'I'm Tolan,' said Spence.

Ortiz kicked him in the belly, and Spence curled up on the floor, clutching at his gut.

'That's a lie,' said Ortiz. 'You ain't Tolan. Before I've finished I'll know exactly who you are, and why you're here. Because one thing I'm sure about, you didn't trick your way into my hacienda just to make a fool of me.'

'I don't know what you're talking about,' said Spence, knowing that the moment he admitted he was a fake he was dead. 'I'm Zeke Tolan. We used to ride together.'

Ortiz kicked him again, and damn near broke Spence's ribs.

'You still say you're Zeke Tolan?'

'Yeah,' said Spence.

'So who the hell is *this*?' asked Ortiz.

Spence looked up, and when his vision had cleared he saw that another person had entered the room.

The man who'd just walked in was the exact image of himself, but with long hair that hung around his head, covering his ears.

It was Zeke Tolan.

Ma Cole had followed Spence's trail, all the way down to the rooming house in that small town a couple of miles south of the border, where Spence had first encountered the Pinkerton man, Harris.

She'd got hold of Zeke Tolan's wanted poster. It was one of those that had a lithograph picture printed on it. Some time ago Tolan had been foolhardy enough to pose for a photograph. Ma Cole had heard of outlaws doing this, and couldn't understand it. Why get your image preserved for eternity? Didn't they realize it meant any lawman who got hold of the picture would know what you looked like? It was stupidity, but if there was one thing Ma Cole had learned in her fifty-three years on this Earth, it was that people were dumb. They just couldn't help themselves.

She showed the wanted poster to the man who

owned the rooming house and said, 'I'm a bounty hunter, and I'm looking for this man. See here, how it says he's a murderer and a bank robber? It's your civil duty to tell me where he went.'

The man was about half Ma Cole's size, and very scared. He'd never heard of a female bounty hunter, but he wasn't about to argue with her. If any woman was up to the task of hunting down outlaws and bringing them to justice, he reckoned it was her.

'He – he didn't call himself Zeke Tolan,' he stammered. 'He called himself Daniel Spence.'

'You see him talk to anybody?'

'Once, I saw him walk out of here with another man.'

'You ever seen this other man before?'

'Y-yes,' said the man. He had seen the other man before. It was only a small town. He'd seen him walking around town with yet another man, older and with grey hair. He told Ma Cole about the grey-haired man. 'He's staying in the Orient Hotel.'

'Much obliged,' said Ma Cole.

When she left, the man wiped the sweat off his face with a kerchief. He didn't know how lucky he'd been. He was one of the few men Ma Cole had ever encountered in her whole adult life who she hadn't felt the need to kill or maim, or at least rough up a little.

Ma found the Orient Hotel, which was a slightly more salubrious establishment a little way down the street. There were velvet drapes over the windows instead of burlap ones, and the cockroaches were a little more discreet.

The man who ran this place wasn't quite so co-operative. 'I don't care who you are, and what you want, I ain't telling you nothing,' he said. He was a big fellow, a little older than Ma, and used to getting his way. He'd been a bare-knuckle champion in his younger days, and had the scars to prove it. He wasn't afraid of any man, and he certainly wasn't scared of any woman, no matter how tough she talked.

He might have told Ma anything she'd wanted to know if she'd asked him in the right way, especially if the request had been accompanied by money, but Ma hadn't been too polite. And she wasn't the kind who handed out bribes if simply beating a man to a pulp got her what she wanted.

'That your final word?'

'It is,' he said. 'Now get out of my hotel.'

Back at the hideout in the canyon she'd picked up a few items she thought she might find useful, and one of those items had been a set of brass knuckles. And while the man had been telling her that he wasn't going to tell her anything, she'd slipped her hand into the pocket of her coat.

She slid her fingers inside the brass knuckles and said, 'That ain't no way to talk to a lady.'

She punched the man in the mouth and sent him crashing back against the wall. He brought his hands up to protect himself, but that didn't help much when Ma swung a low uppercut at his groin.

The man folded, and when he folded she hit him in

the left kidney.

He knelt on the floor, spitting teeth and blood and making a high-pitched keening noise.

She grabbed his right hand, and twisted his fingers back till she heard something snap.

He howled.

Ma kept hold of his fingers and said, 'You ain't finished with me till I tell you you're finished. The man with the grey hair – what was his name?'

'Hubert Jeffries.'

'The man whose picture I showed you, Tolan – he visit him?'

'Yeah.'

'Another man brought Tolan here to meet Jeffries. Who was that?'

'George Harris.' Tears were running down the man's cheeks.

'He stay here too?'

'Yes.'

'Where'd they go when they left here?'

'How the hell should I know?'

Ma figured that if the man knew, he'd tell her.

'Anything else you know about 'em?'

'They were talking about buying a mule.'

Ma paid a visit to the nearest livery stable, where Jeffries and Harris and Tolan had all stabled their horses while they'd been in town.

It turned out they *had* bought a mule. The owner of the livery stable was talkative, lucky for him. He told her that he'd heard the men talking about travelling south, and meeting up with some fellow the grey-haired fellow knew. And then they'd talked about going to the hacienda of Hernando Ortiz.

'Ortiz?' asked Ma.

'*Sí*,' said the man who owned the livery stable, whose white moustache was stained brown by the tobacco he kept chewing and spitting, chewing and spitting. 'Hernando Ortiz. You have not heard of him?'

'No,' said Ma. 'Who is he?'

'He used to be a *bandito*,' said the man. 'But now he is a very rich man, and has powerful friends in the government, and in America. The generals, they give him a little army all of his own to protect him. And everybody is supposed to forget that he was once a *bandito*. This is what happens when you are rich.' He spat tobacco juice at the dirt.

'Where's his hacienda?' asked Ma.

'You got a map?' he asked. 'I will show you.'

'You're sure unlucky,' said the real Zeke Tolan. 'I just happened to be paying a visit on my friend Hernando here. I recently acquired some gold candlesticks that I thought he might pay me for. I know how ol' Hernando loves his gold. And when I turned up, you know what he said? He said, "If you're Zeke Tolan, who the hell is that other sonofabitch?" Of course, I had no idea what he was talking about. Then he looks at me and says, "How do I know he ain't the real Zeke Tolan, and you're the liar?" So we talked some, and I reminded him of a few things that had happened to us, back when we were robbing banks together, and soon enough he was convinced that I'm the real Zeke Tolan. . . . Which still leaves us with the question of who you are. So who are you, boy? And what you doing going round pretending to be me?'

'I ain't saying nothing,' said Spence.

They dragged Spence out of Ortiz's house, because Ortiz didn't want blood all over his nice furniture.

They took him outside and tied him to a wooden post close to the wall that ran around the compound. They tied him so that he was facing the post, his wrists suspended on a kind of hook, and they stripped him down to the waist.

'Bracho's going to whip you,' said Ortiz. 'He's got a bullwhip. When he whips a man they can hear him scream in Oklahoma City. He can flay the skin right off a man's back without so much as working up a sweat. Only problem is, he enjoys it a little too much. I have to make him go easy, otherwise he kills 'em too soon. So I told him to be real gentle with you.'

'I sure appreciate that,' said Spence.

'You're making jokes now,' said Ortiz, 'but pretty soon you'll be crying like a girl, begging me to put a bullet in your brain, to take the pain away.' He lit a fat cigar. 'Before I'm halfway down this cigar, you'll have told me everything I want to know. You might not think so, but you will.'

Ortiz nodded to Bracho.

Bracho swung the bullwhip, and Spence heard it

hiss as the metal-tipped leather snake parted the air.

When the bullwhip cut into his flesh, Spence gritted his teeth and tried hard not to scream.

'You're a brave fellow, whoever you are,' said Ortiz, blowing out tobacco smoke. 'I sure wish we'd have met in some other circumstances. We might even have ridden together.'

'I don't ride with murdering scum,' said Spence.

Ortiz nodded to Bracho, and again the whip hissed through the air and cut a groove in Spence's back.

CHAPTER SEVENTEEN

'My name's Abel Cole,' Spence told Ortiz after the third lash of the bullwhip. 'I came here because people kept mistaking me for Tolan. I heard you and Tolan were old friends. I also heard you had a lot of gold. So I reckoned if I could fool you into thinking I was Tolan, you'd let me into your hacienda, and then I'd figure how I could steal some of it.'

The cicadas had quietened down some. The sky was lightening in the east, the sun about to rise up from behind the mountains.

'I've heard of Abel Cole,' said Zeke Tolan.

'Yeah?' said Ortiz.

'I believe him.'

'You do?'

'It's what I'd do – trick my way in here, try to get at some of your gold.'

'You would?'

'Sure,' said Tolan, laughing.

Ortiz laughed too.

They cut Spence down.

'Take him to the stables,' said Ortiz to the sergeant. 'Tie him up in an empty stall. We'll shoot him in the morning, after breakfast, before you leave.'

'Why not shoot him now?' asked Tolan. 'I'll do it.'

'No,' said Ortiz. 'I'm tired. I want to enjoy it. Besides, I like firing squads. One of my earliest memories is of a man being shot by a firing squad. It always gives me a thrill.'

Tolan shrugged. 'It's your hacienda,' he said. 'Just don't forget to wake me up. I ain't never seen a genuine Mexican firing squad before.'

A couple of the *federales* dragged Spence to the stables and left him tied up in a stall, bound at the wrists and ankles.

Despite the pain from the grooves the whip had cut into his back, he fell asleep. Or passed out. When he woke up again it was daylight, and the horses in the other stalls were restless. He reckoned they could sense he was there among them. Maybe they could smell his blood.

A couple of hours went by. The soldiers would be coming for him soon, he reckoned.

More time passed. He started to wonder what was taking them so long.

Then he heard a yell, and a rifle shot. Somebody

shouted, 'They're up there! They're coming out of the sun!' And then another rifle shot.

Then he heard somebody run into the stables, but it couldn't have been a soldier. The footfalls weren't heavy enough, and whoever was running wasn't wearing boots.

The bolts of the stall door scraped as they were drawn back. The door opened and Rosario ran in.

She had a knife. She knelt in the straw and cut away the ropes from his wrists and ankles.

'What the hell's going on out there?' asked Spence. He couldn't think straight, on account of the pain. And when she tried to help him up he couldn't move at first. His legs and arms were numb. Then the blood started pumping back into them, and that hurt like hell, too.

'The *federales* have gone loco,' she told him. 'It is the opium. The bottle, it had rolled under the bed. After they had taken you away I went to the well when nobody was looking, and poured the opium into the water.'

'I can't bend over to kiss you,' he said. 'My body hurts too much. You'll have to stand on your toes and kiss me.'

So she stood on her toes and kissed him.

She supported him as he staggered to the door of the stable block and looked out into the sunlit quadrangle.

A soldier was firing a rifle up into the sky, a scared

look on his face.

'What's he doing?' asked Spence.

'He thinks devils are flying out of the sun,' she said. 'It is the opium.'

'I thought opium was supposed to make you fall asleep,' said Spence.

'Perhaps it affects different people in different ways,' said Rosario. 'And it depends how much they have drunk, I think. I looked inside the barracks, and all of the other men were lying on their bunks or on the ground, some with their eyes closed, some with their eyes open but staring at nothing. The soldiers, and the men who arrived last night.'

'I guess they'd be Zeke Tolan's gang.'

'Zeke Tolan? You mean, the man people say you look like?'

'Yeah. He turned up here. That's how Ortiz knew I was lying.'

'But I haven't seen anybody who looks like you. I would have noticed.'

'Maybe Tolan's inside the house.'

The soldier had stopped shooting at the sky. Now he just stood there, staring at the sun, watching for more demons or something.

'This opium stuff sure seems to have done what Harris and Jeffries said it would do,' said Spence.

'Harris and Jeffries? They are your friends? The men who are going to arrest Ortiz?'

'That's right,' said Spence. 'We should open the gates and let 'em in.'

Rosario grinned. 'I have already opened the gates,' she said.

Spence peered across the sunlit quadrangle. 'So you have. Seems there ain't anything left for us to do but wait.'

They didn't have to wait long before Harris and Jeffries and their men rode in through the gates.

Spence waved at them from the door of the stables.

Harris came over. 'You did it!' he said. 'You drugged the *federales*!'

'I had help,' said Spence.

A shot came from the barracks, then another and another.

Spence realized he couldn't see Jeffries or the other men anywhere, just their horses.

There were shots from inside the house, and then more shots from the barracks. Then some of Jeffries' Rangers came out of the barracks, soldiers' uniforms draped over their arms.

'What the hell's going on?' asked Spence.

One of the Rangers saw the soldier standing in the quadrangle, staring up at the sky. The soldier had gone back to gibbering about devils. He pointed his rifle at the sun and squeezed the trigger, but didn't seem to realize his gun was out of bullets.

The Ranger laughed, went up to the soldier and shot him through the head.

The Mexican fell lifeless to the ground.

'You said we didn't have to kill anybody!' shouted Spence.

'We did say that, didn't we?' said Harris. He scratched his jaw. 'The thing is, me and Jeffries haven't been quite honest with you.'

CHAPTER EIGHTEEN

'Yeah?' said Spence. 'How's that?'

'I ain't going to bore you with the whole story, and besides, I ain't got time,' said Harris.

More shots came from the house, and the stallion Harris was riding shied and tossed his head and stamped his hoofs.

'Whoa, boy!' said Harris, settling the horse. Then he turned back to Spence. 'You see, I ain't really a Pinkerton man. Used to be, but not any more. They asked me to leave, as it seemed they didn't like the way I got things done. And Jeffries, well he ain't exactly a Texas Ranger either. Never was one, nor were any of his boys.'

'So who are they?'

'Just everyday outlaws, my boy. Now me, I'm a bounty hunter some of the time, but also I like to do a little bank robbing and train robbing and such. These are hard times, my boy, a man's got to diversify.

You understand that, don't you?'

'Just say what you have to say,' said Spence.

'Well, me and Jeffries, we'd heard about a particular train that runs from north of the border, all the way deep into Sonora, and on this train is a whole load of money. US Dollars. All stacked up in neat little piles, and destined for the various government officials and suchlike influential people who help to keep American businesses running smoothly down here.'

'Bribes,' said Spence.

'That's right,' said Harris. 'My, you don't mince your words, do you?'

'I say it as I see it,' said Spence.

'Well, as I say, this train rolls all the way down into Sonora, but it's kind of difficult to rob, on account of all the guards who travel with it. On the Arizona side of the border, the money is guarded by a load of hired guns, but at the border they get off the train, and a load of Mexican *federales* get on and guard it the rest of the way.'

'You mean, these here *federales* who are normally guarding Ortiz?'

'You're a quick one, ain't ya? That's right. Most of the soldiers who usually spend their time guarding Ortiz leave here and spend a couple of days guarding all that money. Now, the plan that Jeffries and I came up with was, we have somebody put opium in the soldiers' drinking water. Then we steal their uniforms, and take their place on the train.'

'And steal the money.'

'And steal the money. We'd planned to get a few *putas* together, send them in here, have one of them pour the opium in the water. . . .'

'Then I came along.'

'You did indeed. When I heard Zeke Tolan was around, I thought maybe I'd do a little bounty hunting on the side, make a little extra money. But you turned out not to be Tolan after all. Then I recalled hearing how Tolan and Ortiz were old acquaintances. Not exactly big buddies, but friendly enough. I reckoned that if you turned up here saying you were good ol' Zeke, he might let you in. And he did.'

'So this wasn't anything to do with taking Ortiz back to America to face justice?'

'Oh, I'll take him back all right,' said Harris. 'He'll be dead, that's all. He's worth as much dead as he is alive, and dead men are less trouble. Bounty hunters learn that real quick.'

Spence said, 'So that story about you and Zeke Tolan growing up together, and you biting off his earlobe – was that a lie too?'

'I bit his earlobe off all right,' said Harris, 'and we grew up in the same town, but I didn't really know him. Only really met him that one time, when we fought, though I'd seen him around a few times. A mean cuss, even when he was a kid. His ma was mean, too. She wasn't ever like a mother to me – I just said that because I thought it sounded good.'

Out in the quadrangle, the so-called 'Rangers' were

stripping off the clothes they'd been wearing and putting on the dead soldiers' uniforms, swopping tunics and boots, finding ones that fitted.

'You shot the soldiers,' said Spence. 'You didn't have to do that. They were drugged anyway. They weren't going to put up any kind of a fight.'

'I haven't shot anybody,' said Harris, almost looking offended. 'The boys have done all the shooting. They dearly love killing people.'

'You're a murdering sonofabitch,' said Spence. 'And so's Jeffries.'

'And you're a fool,' said Harris. 'You know, I could scarce believe how easy it was, convincing you to come down here, pretend you were Zeke Tolan and put the opium in the water. I guess there really is a sucker born every minute, like they say. . . . By the way, who were those fellows who came riding in here last night?'

'That was the real Zeke Tolan and his gang,' said Spence.

Harris laughed. '*Really*? Well, I'll be damned! Small world, ain't it? I reckon that must have made things kinda awkward for you.'

'Yeah,' said Spence. 'Kinda.'

'Guess that explains why you're not looking so healthy this fine morning. This just keeps getting better and better. I can take Zeke Tolan's body back across the border, too.' Harris levelled his rifle at Spence. 'Time to say goodbye, my friend.'

'You gonna kill me?'

'I have to. I can see by the look in your eyes, you ain't going to rest till you get revenge on me and my friend Jeffries, so I reckon I'd better kill you now, otherwise I'll spend the rest of my life looking over my shoulder. And I don't want that. No sir. . . .'

Before Harris could squeeze the trigger, the handle of a knife appeared, jutting out of his throat.

It happened so quick, neither Spence nor Harris rightly knew at first what had happened.

Rosario, supporting Spence with her left arm, still had the knife she'd used to cut the ropes that had bound his wrists and ankles. She'd tucked it into the back of her skirt's waistband, and while Harris and Spence had been talking, she'd reached behind her and taken it out, ready. She'd seen enough men like Harris to know that he wouldn't leave Spence alive.

So when Harris had levelled the rifle at Spence, she'd thrown the knife, and the blade had buried itself deep in Harris's neck.

While Harris was still figuring out what had happened, she got her face up close to the horse's ear and let out a shriek.

The horse shied again and reared up, and Harris toppled from the horse and slammed onto the ground.

Rosario let go of Spence and kicked the rifle out of Harris's grip. She pulled the knife from his throat and plunged it into his heart.

Harris's eyes stared up at the hot blue Mexican sky, and as Spence watched, all the life went out of them.

'How did you learn how to throw a knife?' Spence asked.

'Practice,' said Rosario. 'I know how to do many things.'

He didn't doubt it.

She unfastened Harris's gunbelt, dragged it out from under him, and said to Spence, 'How strong do you feel? You have lost much blood. Will you be able to use the handgun?'

'I'm strong enough to use a gun,' he said. 'Just don't ask me to run anywhere.'

Rosario fixed the gunbelt around his waist, picked up the rifle and said, 'I must tend to your back. We shall go inside the house and find bandages, and alcohol.'

'Yes, ma'am,' said Spence.

They went into the house. There weren't any of Jeffries's men in there, they'd all left. They found a couple of servants in the main room, the room in which Spence and Ortiz had been drinking whiskey the night before. They lay dead, their blood soaking into the fancy rugs.

Rosario led Spence deeper into the house.

They passed the open door of a bedroom, expensively furnished, with a big four-poster bed in it. Ortiz lay on the bed, a gunshot wound in the centre of his forehead. It looked like he'd been killed in his sleep.

There wasn't any sign of the real Zeke Tolan.

They found a kitchen, and a laundry next to it.

'Sit down,' she told him.

139

He sat on a three-legged stool in the laundry.

'Wait here. I shall get alcohol to clean your wounds.'

When she came back she had a bottle of whiskey, one of the bottles Spence had brought with him as a gift for Ortiz.

Rosario tore a strip of cotton from the corner of a cotton bed-sheet, folded it into a pad and poured whiskey onto it. 'This is going to hurt,' she said.

'I could sure do with a shot of that whiskey,' said Spence.

She gave him the bottle and he gulped down a slug of it. Then she cleaned his wound, and it hurt like hell.

'Now I put salt on it,' she said.

'*Salt?* Now wait a minute. . . .'

'It is to stop the wound from getting infected.'

He didn't know how she knew so much about wounds, but he trusted her, so he let her rub salt into the grooves the whip had made, and that hurt like hell, too.

Then she found a jar of honey, and she smeared that over his wounds. 'To keep it clean,' she said.

The honey wasn't so bad.

She tore more strips off the cotton sheets and used them as bandages, wrapping them around his torso. She found a man's shirt that had been washed and dried, and he put it on.

'Now we can get out of here,' said Rosario.

They went back out the way they'd come in, past

Ortiz's bedroom, past the bodies of the servants.

They'd almost made it out of the door when they heard a crash behind them. Spence turned and saw Ortiz's giant bodyguard, Bracho, stumbling through a doorway.

He had a dazed, drugged look in his eyes, and three bullet holes in his gut, his shirt caked with drying blood. Jeffries's men had left him for dead, and now he was staggering around in an opium haze, looking for something to kill.

Bracho scanned the room and saw Spence and Rosario. He let out a weird animal moan and lurched towards them.

With one massive paw, he grabbed Rosario by the neck and lifted her off her feet. Spence drew his six-gun but Bracho swiped at him with his other arm, and Spence felt like he'd been hit with an iron girder. He crashed to the ground and pain coursed through him again, so bad he nearly passed out.

He forced himself back onto his feet.

Bracho pressed Rosario against a wall. She'd dropped the rifle and was scrabbling at his face, scratching at it and pushing her thumbs into his eyes, but nothing would stop him, he kept on crushing her neck.

Spence aimed his six-gun at Bracho's body and squeezed the trigger. But instead of it firing, he heard a *snap* from inside the gun. Spence knew what the sound meant. The hammer spring had busted. The same thing had happened to him about ten years before. When that happened you had to open up the gun and replace the spring, but till you did that the gun was just a lump of metal.

Meanwhile, Bracho carried on throttling Rosario. Her face had turned blue.

Spence pistol-whipped Bracho, but that had no effect.

Rosario's eyes bulged out of their sockets.

On a nearby table stood a big gold candlestick. Spence picked it up and swung the candlestick in a wide, high arc. He brought it down hard on Bracho's skull.

Spence heard the giant's skull split open.

Bracho's grip loosened on Rosario's neck, and she dropped to the floor.

But the huge Mexican wasn't finished yet. Blinded by Rosario's fingers, shot three times and with his skull fractured, he turned and started lashing out at Spence.

Spence swung the candlestick again. This time it smashed into Bracho's temple. The man staggered and fell, crashing to the floor. He lay still.

Spence cradled Rosario in his arms. Her face wasn't so blue now. Her eyes focused on him.

'You all right?' he asked her.

'Is he dead?' she whispered.

'I reckon so.'

Her arm snaked out and wound around his neck. She pulled him towards her and kissed him. Then she said, 'I think we had better leave before something else happens.'

CHAPTER NINETEEN

Jeffries and his fake Texas Rangers had changed into the dead soldiers' uniforms and made their way down to the train depot, three miles away.

This was where the money train would stop, the American hired guns would get off, and the *federales* were supposed to take over guarding all those dollars.

Jeffries had killed Ortiz himself, shooting him while he'd slept. Before leaving the compound, he'd looked around, wondering where Harris was, and found his body lying in the dirt. His throat had been cut and he'd been stabbed in the heart, and both his rifle and his six-gun were missing.

How that had happened he didn't know, and didn't much care. Jeffries and Harris had got along all right, but they'd never really been friends. Jeffries wasn't going to waste time and energy trying to get revenge for Harris's killing, or any of that nonsense.

He had work to do.

Jeffries and his men were tanned from the sun, and

with their *federale* uniforms on, they looked passably Mexican. Enough to fool the American hired guns, anyway.

He watched the hired guns jump off the train as it hissed steam at the tiny makeshift depot, taking on water for the next leg of its journey, deep into Sonora.

The hired guns released their horses from the wagon where they'd been stalled, and climbed onto them to make the return trip north.

One of Jeffries's men was called Calhoun. He was half-Irish, half-Comanche, and he looked about the most convincingly Mexican of all of them. Calhoun also happened to be the one who'd fitted the dead sergeant's tunic best.

The fellow who was evidently in charge of the hired guns saw Calhoun's sergeant's stripes, rode up to him and said, 'It's all yours now, Sergeant.'

'*Muchas gracias, señor,*' replied Calhoun. Which was about as much Spanish as he knew.

The hired gun looked at Calhoun curiously and said, 'What happened to the other sergeant?'

Calhoun said, 'He was killed by Pancho Villa's men, *señor.* It was a great tragedy.'

The man seemed satisfied with that. He nodded and said, 'Good luck.'

Calhoun saluted him, about the sloppiest salute Jeffries had ever seen, but that didn't seem to matter. The man turned his horse around, and the next thing, he and the rest of the hired guns were heading north like they couldn't get out of Mexico fast enough.

Jeffries said to Calhoun, 'Get everybody on the train.'

Five minutes later the locomotive's wheels were turning again, dragging the money south.

Once they got into the mountains, Jeffries and a couple of other men would climb over the coal car to the locomotive. They would kill the engineer and fireman, while somebody else took care of the conductor. Then they'd stop the train, steal the money and ride away.

After they'd divided up all those dollars, Jeffries planned to head to the coast, maybe get a ship down to South America somewhere.

He'd have enough money to live in luxury for a while. He didn't know what the other men intended to do, and didn't care.

That was the plan, anyway.

Everything went just fine till they got into the foothills, and Jeffries was preparing to climb up over the coal car when all hell broke loose.

First there was the explosion. A couple of sticks of dynamite tore up the rails in front of them, and before the engineer could stop the train, the locomotive had hurtled off the track, its iron wheels unable to grip the hard-baked dirt.

Eventually the train came to a halt. Somehow it stayed upright. Jeffries and his men were in the wagon directly behind the coal car, in front of the wagon where the money was. And behind that was the wagon where they'd put the horses.

At first Jeffries thought he was blind, but then he realized his eyes were full of blood. When the train had juddered off the track, he'd been flung across the wagon and smashed his head against a window.

Everybody was on the floor, a jumble of limbs.

A bullet hit the wagon. Then another, and another.

'Somebody's firing at us!' yelled Calhoun.

'That's what I always liked about you,' said Jeffries. 'You're smart.'

If Calhoun knew he was being mocked, he didn't show it.

'They're firing at us to keep us pinned down,' said Jeffries. 'Goddammit, I wish we'd used dynamite. All this tomfoolery about getting somebody to put opium in the water, and getting dressed up as *federales*. Why the hell did I ever agree to it?'

Calhoun wasn't listening. He was crawling up onto one of the bench seats so he could see out of a window. He peered out through the shattered glass, trying to find somebody he could shoot at.

They found him first. Yet another shot rang out, and Calhoun fell back down again, a bullet in his head.

One of the other men screamed, 'We gotta get out of here!'

Jeffries laughed. He pulled out a cheroot, lit it. 'Save your breath, son. We gambled, and we lost. We ain't never getting out of here.'

The next moment something dropped through the

smashed window that Calhoun had just been peering out of.

The object was cylindrical, mud-brown in colour, and had a short fuse that had already burnt most of the way down.

The man screamed.

'If you want to say a prayer,' said Jeffries, 'you better make it a short one.'

Then the dynamite exploded.

FINALE

Spence and Rosario heard the explosions and the gunfire as they were leaving Ortiz's compound, on the horse and mule Spence had ridden in with.

Rosario had stuffed a pair of saddle-bags with gold coins and rings and stuff that she'd found in Ortiz's bedroom.

Ortiz had sure liked his gold.

As Rosario had filled the saddle-bags, Spence had said, 'That's stealing. I don't care much for stealing.'

She said, 'Don't be a fool. For one thing, Ortiz was a thief. Everything he had, he stole from somebody else, and if we wanted to return it, who would we return it to? For another thing, he is dead, and has no family we know of, so who are we stealing it from? And another thing: if we leave it here, who will take it? The Mexican government? The politicians are *bastardos codiciosos*. They will keep it for themselves, and they are rich enough already. Or they will use it to buy more guns and bullets, to kill the people.'

Spence said, 'What does "*codiciosos*" mean? I don't know that word.'

'It means greedy.'

'Oh.'

'So "*bastardos codiciosos*" means greedy bastards.'

'Yeah, I got that.'

Now that he considered her point of view, he reckoned she was right. If anybody else wanted any of Ortiz's gold, there was still plenty of it around, what with his golden statues of naked women and whatever else.

They decided to ride west, towards the coast. They didn't have anywhere in particular they needed to go. Rosario didn't want to go anywhere especially, but Spence still wanted to know what the ocean looked like.

'I've read about it in books,' said Spence. 'But I've never seen it.'

'Nor me,' said Rosario.

As they left the compound they saw a group of women sitting in the dirt. Some of them were crying.

'They are the other women the soldiers took from my village,' said Rosario. 'I am glad they were not killed.' She called out to them in Spanish: 'Go back into the compound and steal anything you can carry, anything you think you can sell. There is much gold. You will be safe, all the soldiers are dead. They cannot harm you.'

A couple of the women looked like they might do just that.

'I can only make the suggestion,' Rosario said to Spence. 'Whether they do it or not is up to them.'

It was then that they heard the explosions.

'I guess that'll be something to do with Jeffries and his men, and that train full of money,' said Spence.

'But their plan was to disguise themselves as *federales*, and get on the train that way,' said Rosario. 'Why would they need to use explosives?'

Spence didn't have an answer to that one.

It was only when they got into the mountains and they encountered the revolutionaries that they found out what the explosions were all about.

The two men appeared on the road in front of them as if they were *fantasmas* who'd just materialized out of the rocks. One moment the road up the mountain had been clear. The next, there they were: two men with sombreros and carbines, and cartridge belts slung across their chests.

'*Detener*,' said one of the men. *Stop*.

So they stopped.

'What do you want?' Spence asked them in Spanish.

'You're American, yes?'

Rosario answered for him. 'He is only half-American. His mother was Mexican.'

Which was a lie, but Spence reckoned she knew what she was doing.

The man who'd spoken looked at him. 'Is that true?'

'Yes,' said Spence.

'What are you doing here?' asked the other man.

'We want to get to the coast,' said Spence.

'Our village was raided by soldiers,' said Rosario. 'We only just managed to get away with our lives, and a few belongings.'

'You were lucky,' said the first man. Then he spotted the blood soaking through Spence's shirt. 'What happened to your back?'

Spence said, 'I got captured by Ortiz's soldiers. You heard of Ortiz?'

The first man nodded. The second man spat on the dirt and said, 'He is a sonofabitch. I would like to kill him.'

'You're too late,' said Spence. 'He's already dead.'

'Really? You killed him?'

Spence was about to say no, he hadn't killed him, but Rosario beat him to it and said, 'Yes. My man, he killed Hernando Ortiz. And Ortiz's bodyguard – the giant, Bracho – my man killed him, too.'

The men's eyebrows shot straight up towards their sombreros. 'Bracho? That big bastard? You killed him also?'

'Yeah,' said Spence. 'He attacked my woman, so I split his head open.'

The men liked that. They took turns shaking Spence's hand.

Rosario said, 'What were the explosions we heard?'

'We have stolen the money the rich American businessmen sent by train to bribe the politicians,' said the second man.

151

'Just the two of you?' asked Spence.

They both laughed. 'No,' said the first man. 'There were a hundred of us. The others are resting now. We are sentries. We are part of Pancho Villa's Division of the North. We derailed the train and stole the money. Now we can buy guns and bullets, and food for the people.'

Rosario said, 'Pancho Villa? I have heard of him. He is a great man.'

'The greatest man who ever lived!' said the first man.

The second man agreed. 'He will wipe Mexico clean of corruption, and once more it shall be a fit place for ordinary people to live.'

'Sounds good to me,' said Spence. 'What did you do with the soldiers who were guarding the money?'

The first man shrugged. 'We killed them, of course.'

The second man said, 'It is what they deserved.'

Spence said, 'Do you mind if we continue on our way? We are going to the coast. I want to see the ocean. I've never seen it.'

The men let them pass. As they passed, the first man said, 'I have seen the ocean. It is not so great.'

It was about an hour after that when Rosario said, 'The man Zeke Tolan, who they said you looked like – what do you think happened to him? You think he is dead?'

'Probably,' said Spence. 'But I reckon we'll never know for sure.'

*

A little while after that, Zeke Tolan crawled out of the cupboard he'd been hiding in when he'd heard the shooting.

Ortiz had let Tolan sleep in the same room that Spence had been given.

When Tolan had entered the room he'd found the sheets were rumpled. The fellow who'd pretended to be him had been with a woman. Tolan could smell her.

He didn't much like the idea of sleeping on those sheets. Tolan reckoned he'd rather sleep in a pigsty than on sheets where a man and a woman had been together. He tore them off the bed, threw them in a corner and found clean sheets in a big old fancy dark-wood cupboard. He put the new sheets on the bed, kicked off his boots, stripped off his dirt-caked clothes and lay down. It wasn't long before he was asleep.

He was woken up by gunfire.

First it was outside the house, then it was inside.

It sounded like a whole gang of men were going from room to room, shooting anybody they found.

He leapt off the bed, grabbed his six-gun and hid in the cupboard.

When the men got to his room, they looked inside, saw nobody, and went away again.

He figured they must be pretty dumb. They must have seen his clothes lying on the floor, and the empty holster, but they didn't even think to look in the cupboard. He'd had his finger on the trigger of his six-gun, ready to blast the head off any man who opened the cupboard door, but nobody did.

Tolan waited, listening, wondering if they'd come back into the room, but they didn't.

Eventually everything went quiet.

He heard talking. He heard a fight, then more talking, then silence again.

It was only when he was certain there wasn't any other living person still in the house that he emerged from the cupboard.

He pulled on his clothes and walked around the house.

Ortiz was dead. It looked like he'd been shot in his sleep.

Ortiz's bodyguard, Bracho or whatever, was dead too. Shot and with his head stoved in. There were a whole lot of other people dead, too.

He walked around the compound. Ortiz's soldiers were dead, and all of Tolan's own gang.

How it had happened, he couldn't figure. It must have been a whole goddamn army who'd attacked the place. Revolutionaries, Tolan reckoned. Had to be. A couple of hundred of Pancho Villa's Division of the North.

It looked like Ortiz's soldiers had been stripped of their uniforms. He couldn't work that one out, not at all.

And how come he couldn't see any dead revolutionaries? How had they been able to kill all of the men inside the compound without any of the revolutionaries also getting killed?

It didn't make any kind of sense to him.

He was thirsty. Since arriving at Ortiz's hacienda, Tolan had drunk nothing except whiskey. But now he needed water. He drew some out of the well and drank about a pint of it, and poured the rest of the bucket over his head.

He started back to the house. He wanted to eat food, drink coffee, sit and think about what had happened, and what he should do next.

He'd just about reached the house when everything started to go weird, like he was drunk, but different somehow. Suddenly he was on the ground, and he wasn't sure how he'd got there. Then his mind started to drift.

A while later, it could have been seconds, it could have been hours, it could have been whole decades, he didn't know, the sky darkened and he was looking up at the night sky full of stars, and he thought he was one of them. Then the sky turned blue again, and the sun was burning his skin.

Then a shadow fell across him, and that was good, the sun wasn't burning him any more.

A voice that could have been a man's or a woman's said, 'I'm going to kill you, Tolan!'

Then she was pointing a big gun at his face, and that's the last he knew.

Ma Cole looked down at the man she'd shot.

Now she studied him properly, she could tell it

wasn't the right man. They looked pretty much alike, but this wasn't the same man she knew as Zeke Tolan. This man was fuller-faced, and his hair was longer. The man she knew as Zeke Tolan wouldn't have been able to grow his hair that long in so short a time.

She'd shot the wrong man.

She swore, and spat in the dead man's face.

'Sonofabitch,' she said.

After several days' ride they reached the ocean.

Spence stood on a bluff overlooking the water. It was a bright day, no cloud, and the sea was calm. The blue of the water lay under the blue of the sky, and Spence couldn't get over how big it was.

'It's even bigger than Texas,' he said.

Rosario said, 'Now what do you want to do?'

Spence said, 'What do *you* want to do?'

She said, 'There's a revolution starting here. And I have little interest in America. Perhaps we should try somewhere else. Let us find a port, and a ship.'

They headed south along the coast till they found a port.

It was in the port town that Ma Cole finally caught up with Danny Spence.

Ma Cole was still in pain from the gunshot wound in her leg. But the pain of the wound was nothing compared to the pain of losing her sons. Most other people would be in bed recuperating, but her hatred for the man she knew as Zeke Tolan, who she blamed for all her misfortune, spurred her on.

She'd followed Spence's trail from the *hacienda*, and when she had discovered he'd been heading due west towards the coast, she reckoned that sooner or later he would turn up in this port town, the largest town for miles.

She'd travelled faster than Spence and Rosario, overtaking them while they slept in a cave only a hundred yards from the road, and arrived the night before they did.

He'll board a ship, she thought. *Why else would he head for a port?*

So she hung around, watching for Tolan.

When she saw them – Tolan riding a horse, the woman riding a mule – she pulled a Colt .45 from under her coat and stepped out into the street.

Ma didn't want to challenge him to a duel, she wanted him dead. She had no objection to shooting somebody in the back, she'd done that before, but she wanted Tolan to know who was about to kill him.

As the man and the woman passed by, she shouted, 'Zeke Tolan!'

She already had the gun pointed at him.

The street was full of people. A woman close by, walking along the boardwalk with her children, screamed when she saw Ma, and bundled her offspring into a store.

Spence turned in his saddle and saw Ma Cole aiming a six-gun at him, and he couldn't believe it. He'd been certain that the good people of Paradise

Flats had hanged her, yet here she was, bigger and meaner than ever, and looking like she was one second away from killing him.

The gunshot was very loud, and Spence thought, *This is it. After everything I've been through, I'm dead.* But somehow he wasn't dead. He was still sitting on the horse, and unless he was mistaken, he hadn't been shot.

Ma Cole had been shot, though. A hole had appeared in her shirt front, just above her heart. Assuming she had a heart. But she stayed on her feet, and she was still pointing her gun at him.

There was another gunshot, and this time a hole appeared in the centre of her chest. She looked down and saw the blood spreading across her shirt.

Then there was a third gunshot, and this time the bullet punched a hole in the bridge of her nose.

The gun dropped from Ma's fist and she crashed to the dirt.

Spence twisted around a little more and saw Rosario holding a zinc-plated Smith & Wesson, a wisp of smoke rising from the muzzle.

'Where'd you get that?' he asked her.

'I picked it up before we left the *hacienda*,' she said. 'Pretty, isn't it? It was Ortiz's.'

A Mexican gentleman in a fancy suit came up to them and said in English, 'I saw everything. The woman tried to kill you, and you killed her first, fair and square. There shall not be any trouble.'

Spence tipped his hat and said, 'Much obliged to

you, but it might be best if we stuck around and explained things to a lawman.'

The man grinned. 'You do not need to concern yourselves. I *am* a lawman.'

So that was all right.

Spence and Rosario found a place where they got a fair price for some of the gold coins they'd taken from Ortiz's place, then they carried on towards the quayside. A ship looked like it was getting ready to sail. A man was leaning out over the rail, watching cargo being loaded. Spence called up to him and said in Spanish, 'Pardon me, but are you the captain?'

The man answered in English, 'I certainly am. What can I do for you?'

'Can you tell me where you're bound for?' asked Spence.

'First we sail to Papeete, on the island of Tahiti. Then it's full steam ahead to Australia. Will that do for you?'

Spence consulted with Rosario a moment, and then asked, 'Do they speak English in Australia?'

'Better than anyone else in world,' said the captain. 'Including the English.'

'Do they have cattle ranches there?'

'They do. Except we call them cattle stations.'

Spence said, 'Could you tell us how much it would cost us to travel with you to Australia?'

The captain told him, and they consulted again, and decided the fee was reasonable. Spence asked, 'Do you have room for us on board?'

'I have one cabin with two bunks,' said the captain. 'But only if you're married. I'm very particular about that.'

Spence and Rosario consulted again, and Rosario asked, 'Is it correct that you can officiate in a marriage on board your ship? Like a priest?'

'That's right, ma'am. I can marry people, soon as we're at sea.'

So Spence and Rosario consulted one more time, and decided that's what they'd do.